The Secrets of Grindlewood

OTHELIA'S ORB

JACKIE BURKE

LINDON BOOKS

First published by Lindon Books in 2017,
9 Raheen Park, Bray, Co. Wicklow.
Web: www.grindlewood.com
Email: jackieburke@grindlewood.com

Paperback	ISBN: 978 1 911013 92 1
eBook – mobi format	ISBN: 978 1 911013 93 8
eBook – ePub format	ISBN: 978 1 911013 94 5
CreateSpace edition	ISBN: 978 1 911013 95 2

Produced by Kazoo Independent Publishing Services
222 Beech Park, Lucan, Co. Dublin
www.kazoopublishing.com

Kazoo Independent Publishing Services is not the publisher of this work. All rights and responsibilities pertaining to this work remain with Lindon Books.

Cover design by Andrew Brown
Cover and internal illustrations © Fintan Taite 2017
Printed in the EU

About the Author

Jackie grew up with her sister and three brothers in Dublin. An avid reader and writer since her school days, she only recently began writing children's stories, having dreamed of doing so for quite some time. *Othelia's Orb* is the fifth book in the hugely popular *Secrets of Grindlewood* series.

Grindlewood is inspired by all that Jackie loves in nature: gardens, forests, wildlife, cats and dogs, and of course magic! Reading, hill walking and baking are just a few of her many hobbies. Jackie divides her time between writing and giving creative writing workshops to children and adults in schools and libraries around the country. She lives with her husband in Bray, County Wicklow. They share their home with a big fluffy cat called Millie.

Other books in The Secrets of Grindlewood series

The Secrets of Grindlewood (Book 1)

The Secret Scroll (Book 2)

The Queen's Quest (Book 3)

Zora's Revenge (Book 4)

'A classic tale to delight readers aged 8–12'
– Sue Leonard, author and journalist

Contents

Chapter One

OLD SECRETS

Queen Wanda sat alone in her private chamber. She stared at the book lying open on her lap, thinking but not reading any more. *The Book of Prophecies* was for the queen's eyes only, though occasionally her augurers had visions of the prophecies within it.

What she had read confirmed her fears. Othelia's Orb was not a myth; it really did exist and it contained a great mystery, an unknown source of power. She sensed that the children and Timber had already found it, but she was glad they were keeping it a secret. Spies had caused trouble before, and the queen was sure there were more, waiting patiently for the orb's location to be revealed.

The prophecy foretold how Timber was the only

one who could reach the orb, and determine its path, but although she was queen, Wanda was not permitted to influence him. So it was written. 'I must trust him to do the right thing,' she thought. 'And what of this great battle the prophecy spoke of? Will our magic be restored in time? Will Zora and Worfeus unite against us?' And even more importantly, she wondered, who would win out in the end?

Without finding the answers, Wanda closed the book and put it away in her private vault. She paced the chamber long into the night, thinking of how she had involved the *worthy* in so much danger.

Early on Saturday morning, Jamie and Jemima were woken by hammering.

'What's Dad up to now?' asked Jamie as he ran downstairs after his sister. The children were beginning to think their father had been affected by magical memory mist – so much of it had been used after the last two quests.

Fortunately, their father had not gone crazy. Greg simply wanted to know everything about his great-uncle George, who he had never met and who had left him the big house with the huge, wild garden. The family had redecorated the house when they moved in, but the cellar and the attic had not been fully explored or tidied. After his latest discussion with the family's solicitor, Herbert Peabody, Greg was keen to examine both.

Boxes and crates were piled to one side, cupboards pulled down, floorboards taken up, and he had even prised a few bricks out of the walls to see if anything was hidden behind them. When he finally stopped and looked around, Greg noticed that the cellar was smaller than he expected; there was another wall that wasn't on the original drawings. He hammered at it while he waited for an engineer he knew to come and take a look.

'I'm not sure you should be doing that,' said Gloria. 'That extra wall could be holding up the kitchen!'

'Why would anyone put a wall right there?' said Greg. 'It only makes the cellar smaller. There has to be something behind it.'

Gloria shrugged her shoulders and headed back upstairs to check for any new cracks in the kitchen.

Jamie and Jemima were keen to take a look in the cellar, and hurried past their mum on the way down.

'Find anything, Dad?' asked Jamie.

'Papers, mostly,' said Greg. 'I put them in those boxes over there. Some were hidden behind false panels in the walls, as well as under those floorboards.' Greg pointed to the boards he had pulled up. 'I don't know why anyone would put a false floor in a cellar of all places. And then there's this wall. What do you make of it?'

Their thoughts were interrupted by the doorbell. Luke and Abigail had arrived. Gloria let them in and sent them down to join the others.

A few minutes later, the doorbell rang again. This time it was the engineer who was going to examine the strange wall. Greg came up, explained the situation, then led him down the narrow staircase. Leaving the engineer to do his work, Greg asked the children to follow him to the attic, where he wanted to take a look at more old trunks and boxes. 'It's time we sorted this house from top to bottom and put everything in its proper place.'

The four children were excited to rummage through all the old stuff in the attic, and hoped they would find something interesting.

The first few boxes contained more of George's old

business ledgers and accounts books – boring. Three crates were full to the brim with antique toys and books – definitely more fun – and two other trunks had old-fashioned clothes folded and piled up neatly inside. Everything was dusty and smelled old.

Jemima was rooting through the old clothes when she found a small decorated diary in a coat pocket. 'Dad, can I take this to the fairy house?' she asked. 'Oh, and this one?' She picked up another small book from the book crate. Taking a quick look inside, she saw it was another diary but the handwriting was different.

'And this?' said Jamie, holding up a tiny notebook with a tatty black cover. It was hardly bigger than his hand.

'Hmm, what's that?' muttered Greg. He was trying to read some of the ledgers in the dusty light. 'Can't read this properly in here. OK, enough dust. Down we go. I should check on the engineer.' He snapped a thick ledger shut, sending up another puff of dust, turned off the light, and they all went downstairs.

The children went out to the fairy house with their finds, followed quickly by Timber and Teddy. The four friends gathered around the little table, Timber on the floor beside them, his head on Jamie's knee.

Teddy curled up on Jemima's lap as she opened the decorated diary first. 'This belonged to Great-great-aunt Gemima,' she said. 'She wrote exactly what Professor Allnutt told us, how she traded gold for magic. And here,' said Jemima, pointing to the handwriting, 'she says it brought nothing but woe.'

'Uh oh!' said Jamie.

'She regretted what she did,' continued Jemima, 'especially as George had been so kind to her and her son, after her husband died of pneumonia.'

'Grim,' said Luke.

'Oh, that's a pity,' said Jemima. 'She didn't write much more.'

Jamie opened the black book. It was written in a strange scrawl. 'What's this, more witch language?'

'I don't think so,' said Abigail, taking a look.

'What then?' asked Jamie.

'It could be some other magical language, but not witch,' said Abigail. 'I'm learning about all the different languages of magical people at the moment.'

'There are more?' asked Luke.

'Lots,' said Abigail.

'Where did George get a notebook written in

a magical language?' said Jemima. 'Could he have written it himself?'

'Only magical people can learn magical languages,' said Abigail.

'Timber can too,' said Jamie.

'That was a special enchantment by the queen,' said Luke.

'Maybe the notebook belonged to someone else, but somehow George got hold of it,' said Abigail, turning it over in her hands before flipping the pages.

The other three thought about that, as they watched her eyes scanning the strange script. Abigail had a way of saying things that turned out to be true. They wondered what she was thinking right now. Did she *know* something?

Timber growled under the table. He didn't like the smell coming from the black book. He stood up and put his paws on the table, and leaned towards the other diary. He nosed it excitedly, preferring the scent.

'You want us to look at this one?' asked Jemima, picking it up. She turned the cover over. There was an inscription inside. 'This was George's diary, his name and address are on it.' She turned to the next page. 'The first entry is from 1880!'

'Oh, skip to the interesting bits,' said Jamie.

16th July, 1880

I have been extremely fortunate in my business dealings over the last few years and accumulated enough money to begin work on this wonderful house in the magical place that is Grindlewood.

14th September, 1885

My business continues to do very well, and I have even been paid in gold. This is most unusual, but I trust all is in order and I will note down everything, just in case.

27th April, 1886

Deepest sadness. My dear brother Geoffrey has died of pneumonia, aged only thirty-six. He leaves a wife and young son in my care.

22nd March, 1887

This gold troubles me. Where did it come from? How many lumps can I turn into cash without it appearing suspicious? I think I am being followed. I must lock the gold away and live off a modest income for a while. My brother's widow, Gemima, and their son Geoffrey II have settled in with me. I have sworn Gemima to secrecy about the gold. Geoffrey is away at boarding school most of the time, and knows nothing of the matter.

'There's a lot more,' said Jemima.

The others nodded to her to read on.

13th November, 1890

Gemima is idle while Geoffrey is away at school and I am busy with my work. I worry when she wanders off on long walks alone.

30th November, 1895

To my horror, Gemima has confessed to a deal with an unscrupulous character, a goblin named Krool. He has taken advantage of her gentle nature and agreed to give her magic in exchange for gold. Alas, the scoundrel has persuaded her to steal from me! How could she have been so foolish? And I never knew goblins were real ...

7th August, 1899

Gemima has a kind and generous heart, and is careful not to reveal her gift of magic to those she helps. But I fear there may be a terrible price to pay for this folly. I refuse to let her grant me any magical favour. I am uneasy about it.

19th February, 1901

My fears are realised! Two dead goblins are in my cellar. I believe they were after the rest of my gold. Gemima recognised one as Krool. Perhaps the other was his accomplice, or even his killer.

23rd February, 1901

We cannot go to the police with a tale of goblins, magic and gold, and we dare not touch the bodies either. Gemima tried to make the two goblins disappear, but spell after spell failed. Eventually, she managed to raise a wall that would hide the two intruders. How I rue the day I accepted gold in payment, tempting these villains to enter our lives.

10th January, 1903

Gemima has taken to her bed. This dreadful goblin business has made her ill. We have been living in fear for two years now.

16th May, 1903

Doctors are still baffled as to what ails Gemima. She does not improve. Even her own magic cannot heal her.

23rd January, 1904

Dear Gemima has passed away. I believe she was doomed the day she accepted the goblin's gift, and it finally killed her.

2nd September, 1905

Geoffrey writes to say he has settled well in Australia.

'There's a big gap and then this,' said Jemima.

9th May, 1950

I am living far too long, though in good health. Perhaps Gemima gave me a gift without telling me – the gift of long life. But it is lonely living so long while I watch everyone I know and love pass away.

'Then another big gap until this:'

1st January, 1995

I am now a ridiculous age, which I must lie about as no one would believe me. Perhaps long life was not a gift from Gemima after all, but part of that goblin's curse.

16th November, 1999

Geoffrey's grandchildren are living in different parts of the world. I never see them, but given my strange history and age, perhaps it is best. The horses are gone. I only have my beagle to keep me company now, dear old Brigadier.

'Everything is true,' said Jemima. 'Gemima's deal with the goblins, George's success as a business man, that he lived to be a great age, and that he kept horses and beagles here.'

'It tells us something more,' said Luke. 'Those goblins' bodies might still be in the cellar.'

Back in the main house, the engineer had finished his inspection and was about to leave.

'It's a strange place to put a wall,' he said, as Greg opened the front door to let him out. 'But it's not supporting anything, so you can knock it down if you wish.'

'Very good,' said Greg. 'And here's the man who will help me do just that. Hello, Arthur.'

'Hello, Greg,' said Luke's father, hopping out of his truck. 'I'm ready when you are.'

Arthur carried in some tools he had brought for the job and the two men quickly got to work. It took most of the afternoon to clear a hole big enough to climb through, and with all the debris and dust, it was difficult to see anything.

The four children hovered near the door, Timber beside them. They wondered if anything mentioned in the diary might still be there, or if somehow the dead goblins had all vanished like George hoped they would.

'Well,' said Greg, 'let's see what this mystery is all about.'

'Mystery?' muttered Jamie.

Luke nudged him with his elbow.

'Do you boys know something we don't?' asked Arthur, spotting the nudge.

'How could we, Dad?' said Luke. 'We just thought we might find treasure or something.'

'Time to find out,' said Greg.

It took a moment for their eyes to adjust as they stepped through the gap and looked into the gloom. Timber sniffed around, snorting occasionally when the dust tickled his nose.

Gloria joined them. With the help of a bright torch, she quickly spotted paintings just inside the gap where they had broken through and began looking through them. There were portraits of George, his younger brother Geoffrey and his wife, Gemima, and their son, Geoffrey II. There were landscape paintings of the area before and after the house was built. Great-aunt Gemima looked very pretty in some portraits, but her expression in others was frightful, even ill-looking.

'Peabody said she died of an unknown illness,' said

Greg. 'That might explain why she looked so different.'

'Your great-uncle George looked very jolly,' said Gloria.

'Yes, but look at that one.' Greg showed her a smaller portrait. 'His expression changed too.'

'He was probably worried when she became ill,' said Gloria.

'Perhaps,' said Greg, replacing the painting, 'or maybe he was worried about some business matter. His ledgers look a bit odd. He certainly made a lot of money, but I can't see where all of it went. He didn't spend much once he finished this house.'

'Maybe he gave it away,' said Gloria, 'or he might not have recorded everything. After all, it was a long time ago. Things were done differently then.'

'Indeed they were,' said Greg. He frowned. 'All right, everyone, that's more than enough dust for today.'

Timber barked loudly, his protective bark.

'That sounds like trouble,' said Jamie, glancing at Luke.

'I hope we don't have more giant rats!' said Gloria.

'Not a chance,' said Greg. 'This room has been sealed for a long time, by the looks of it. Come on,

Timber, out you go. Time to lock up.'

The children reluctantly left. They wanted to look around on their own. Timber bounded past them on the stairs on the way up. Dougal and Teddy had come in from the garden and were waiting for him in the kitchen.

'Uh oh,' said Dougal, 'we know that look.'

'You found trouble, didn't you?' said Teddy.

'Yes,' said Timber. 'Gather everyone in the garden, right away.'

Over in the darkest corner of the cellar, a few gnarled bones peaked out from under the rubble.

Chapter Two

TROUBLE RETURNS

Timber trotted over to the animals. They were waiting anxiously beside the kennel.

'Is there news of Zora?' asked Norville, trundling up last.

'Or Worfeus?' asked Eldric.

'No, it's something else altogether,' Timber said quietly.

The animals and birds leaned closer to hear every word.

'Greg opened up part of the cellar that has been closed off for over a century,' Timber went on. 'It was dark and full of strange smells, but I found something very disturbing – bones. I've never smelled bones like those before. Greg called us out before I could see them.'

'That's not good,' muttered Dougal.

'In all my time here, I've never heard anything about bones,' said the Brigadier.

'There was a mention of dead goblins in one of George's diaries,' said Timber.

'Oh, this is bound to lead to more trouble,' said Norville.

'What'll we do?' asked Teddy.

'I want to take another sniff around,' said Timber. 'The children want to get in and look too, but their father locked the door.'

'We don't want anyone finding the bones before we do,' said Oberon, 'especially if they belong to goblins. It could be dangerous.'

'Greg and Gloria might call the police if they find bones in their house,' said Sylvie.

'And there's very little magic left to cover up something as big as this,' said Teddy.

'I'll let you know when I hear more,' said Timber. 'In the meantime, keep your noses alert for anything that doesn't smell right.'

The pets went about their business and Timber followed the children into the fairy house again. Teddy went on patrol with the other cats and the foxes.

In the fairy house, the children had lots of books spread out all over the floor and piled up on the table. Timber barked at the *History of Magic* book. It was growing again, updating itself in bursts every few days. It was the one book the children knew contained everything about Grindlewood, past and present, though most of it was written in ancient witch language. They wondered if there was something in there about Zora and Worfeus' plans, Othelia's Orb, and now perhaps something about goblins in their cellar. The problem was, it might only be written in the language they couldn't understand.

'Maybe we just aren't meant to see it,' said Abigail. Everyone looked at her, wondering what she meant this time.

'You mean more secrets?' said Jemima.

'Part of that book is written in the oldest of witch languages that even most magical people don't speak or read any more,' said Abigail. 'It's a way of recording history but keeping it very secret, especially the really bad stuff.'

'Well, whatever it says, we can't read the bits we want to read,' said Jamie. 'It's so unfair. We're just waiting and wondering what's going to happen while at the same time, Zora and Worfeus must be making plans. We know everyone wants Othelia's Orb, even though we're the only ones who know where it is, but now there's the cellar problem. There could be goblin bones or goblin gold, or both, down there. We have to find out before anyone else does. And by the way, I'm pretty sure Timber found something.'

Timber barked his 'yes' bark.

'You're right,' said Luke. 'We're stuck. We can't defend Grindlewood from powerful people like Zora and Worfeus on our own. We need the Wandeleis to be ready with their magic at full strength, but it hasn't even been renewed yet. This is such a pain!'

'That's not everything,' said Abigail.

The others looked at her. What on earth had they forgotten?

'Wandeleis aren't *allowed* to attack,' said Abigail. 'We can only defend ourselves when enemies attack us.'

'So that's why nothing is happening,' said Luke.

'Wait a minute,' said Jamie. 'We have to *wait* for the Worfagons to attack?'

Abigail looked as uneasy as she felt. 'Granddad said it's true,' she said. 'I found it in *Magical Learning*, Volume 93.'

'But that gives the enemy the advantage,' cried Jamie.

'I know,' said Abigail. 'An ancient queen, Queen Cassandra, mastered the famous willow wand long ago, but she used it to attack the Worfagons without cause. It was the start of a terrible war.'

'So *both* sides made mistakes in the past,' said Jamie.

'Big ones,' said Abigail. 'The augurers of the time said that the Ancients would insist on a punishment, as well as demanding a promise from the Wandeleis to never launch an attack on other wizards or warlocks again, or face dire consequences.'

'Queen Wanda hinted at that before,' said Luke. 'You remember, when she was telling us we are the *worthy,* and how we have to help them make amends. Now we know what she really meant.'

The mood had gone from impatient to spooked. A noise broke their thoughts when the big history book suddenly stopped expanding with a loud POP, and fell over.

The conversation returned to the problem of the orb.

'Where else could we put it that would be as safe as where it is?' asked Jamie.

'Hard to say,' said Luke, with a loud sigh.

'It looks like glass,' said Jemima. 'Wherever we put it, we must be sure it won't break.'

'An Invisibility chest would work,' said Abigail, 'but Granddad has used one and Queen Wanda has the other.'

Timber put his head on his paws and growled. He had heard this conversation before and it was going nowhere fast. He wasn't happy leaving the orb where they had found it, lying beneath Worfeus' old lair in the forest. Now that the warlock was back, there was a chance he might visit his old haunts, find the entrance to the Pyramid Tomb at the back of the lair, and then follow the passageway that led to the orb. If Worfeus got his hands on the orb, it could only bring disaster.

Now they had the problem of the bones as well.

With so many troubles looming, neither the children nor Timber felt ready to tell anyone they had found the orb, not even Queen Wanda. She was so concerned about more spies, their meetings were held in whispers and kept very short. Any mention of the orb would be risky.

After a long silence, the children agreed once again that the orb would remain where it was.

Since the summer, the two girls had been taking spell lessons with the fairies, and wizards were training the boys in fencing and archery.

Jemima was thrilled she could do a little magic, and her spells were now as good as any novice witch. In contrast, spell-casting was not Abigail's favourite subject. Instead she preferred art and restoration. The fairies had remarked on her exceptional skill as they watched her restore *The Book of Enchantments.*

As soon as the school term ended in late June, and just after Luke's eleventh birthday, the boys had begun their training with the wizards. Jamie had finally hung up his old wooden sword on the wall of the fairy house. It had served him well, magically turning to steel when he needed it to, but the time had come to train with real weapons. Gorlan's sword and shield made Jamie feel like a real Wandelei knight.

Luke was learning how to control Hector's bow using his new gold-tipped arrows. It was more difficult than he expected, but he was doing well. The queen often asked for his help with a very intricate puzzle, one that might hold clues about the orb and the inevitable battle for its possession. To their dismay, however, the final pieces led to even more puzzles within the giant one, and they were beginning to wonder if they would ever get to the bottom of it.

Every Saturday the children had their magical learning lesson with Professor Allnutt. This particular morning, they had a few questions for Abigail's granddad.

'Professor, when this Worfagon attack comes, how will we keep our parents out of it?' asked Jamie.

'We don't want them to be mesmerised too often,' said Jemima. 'It might make them go all weird and maybe even stay that way.'

'I've arranged for Greg to start work on a new project as chief carpenter at the local mill,' said Thaddeus. 'One of my old wizard friends will make sure he has very little time to be near any magical events. As for school, you may have to attend now and then if our magic can't hide the fact that you aren't really there. But rest assured, Esther will keep the school enchanted for as long as her magic will allow.'

'But the magic is weakening all the time,' said Abigail.

'Mrs Emerson will be close by to help out,' said

Thaddeus, 'and Esther will bring magic muffins and herbal chocolate to the teachers and pupils in case anything needs to be, eh, disguised.'

The children didn't looked convinced.

'They will use their last drops of magic to keep the school thinking that the four of you are still in attendance,' Thaddeus added. 'But *only* when the witching hour arrives, not before. You still have to do some normal lessons as well, for a little while longer.' He beamed at each of them, but his magical gold tooth didn't sparkle like it used to.

'So that's what "witching hour" means,' muttered Luke.

Jamie sighed loudly and looked cross, but he said nothing.

'What about Mum?' asked Jemima. 'She works at home most of the time.'

'Esther's sister, Tamara, and her friends are teaching Gloria how to grow medicinal herbs. They'll be visiting other gardens to see how it's done. The witches will keep her busy and safe at all the right times. Those extra herbs will come in handy.'

'And my parents?' asked Luke.

'One of your new farm hands is a wizard,'

said Thaddeus. 'He'll take care of everything on Meadowfield Farm.'

'Oh,' said Luke, wondering which one of the new farm labourers could be the wizard. 'No memory mist, then.'

'A little bit may be required now and then, but we'll keep it to a minimum,' said Thaddeus. He decided to finish the lesson a little early to avoid any more awkward questions. 'That's all for today. I'll see you next Saturday, if not before.'

While the children were out, Timber had been thinking about the orb again. By the time they returned, he had made up his mind to tell Queen Wanda they had found it. He was even more certain it was the right thing to do when he heard the first message from the new butterflies. They landed on his head with a warning.

We are Evie, Edith and Elle,
We have a troubling message to tell.
Double trouble has doubled once more,
You will face more danger than ever before!

The butterflies flew to the children next. As soon

as they received the message, they agreed to visit the queen immediately. Abigail took out the DimLock and whisked them off to the Eastern Woods.

They repeated the message to the queen, and then Timber barked in witch language, telling her that they had found the orb.

'I expected as much,' the queen whispered, also in witch language. 'But tell no one else, Timber. I feel even these hallowed woods have eyes and ears we cannot trust.'

Timber had hoped she would advise them what to do, whether to leave the orb where it was or move it somewhere else, but instead it was to remain another secret. The queen had once told him he would know what to do when the time came, but he didn't know what to do, and surely this was the time when he needed to know? Or perhaps the queen had been referring to something else. Either way, Timber felt uneasy.

Wanda was troubled too. She felt Timber should know more of the prophecy about him, but she was worried how Jamie would react if she told him too.

The queen's hunch was right. Jamie was already feeling irritable. He hated not knowing what the queen was saying to his dog. 'We were hoping the butterflies, or someone, might tell us a bit more about what's going to happen, and when,' he said, a little testily. 'It's hard to prepare when we know so little.'

'The Grindlewood butterflies are magical beings,' said Wanda. 'They will warn us of danger when they dream of it. Pay close attention, no matter how simple or confusing their messages may seem. No one else will be able to tell us anything about the orb, and we found very little in the puzzle. Othelia's Orb has been a mystery for a long time.'

'What do *you* think about this orb?' asked Luke, suspecting that the queen knew more than she was saying.

'It is said to have immense power, including bewitching powers,' said Wanda carefully. 'I have heard that the orb itself decides who to enchant, who to trust, and who to destroy.'

'Sounds like the orb has secrets,' said Jemima. 'Scary secrets.'

'I know you have all been working hard,' said the queen. 'But I want you to return to school after mid-term and continue your magical learning and training at the weekends. Despite all the protections on your school, your parents and the village, it is important that we save our last drops of magic for emergencies. It won't be for long.'

Timber growled and the children looked uneasy.

'If you remain at school a while longer,' said Sparks, 'it will help us save what little magic we have left. We have to hold out until *The Book of Darkness* is ready, and our magical reserves are running low.'

'We cannot waste magic *pretending* you are at school when you could actually be there,' added Flint, flustered as usual. 'You do understand?'

The children didn't answer, though the message was clear.

'When the time comes,' said Wanda, 'we will need the *worthy* by our side and with us until the end of the battle.'

'Have you any idea when it will start?' asked Luke.

'In their visions, our augurers have seen illness and argument in Mord Manor,' said the queen. 'The Worfagons are not ready to attack us, and hopefully our magic will be restored before they do.'

'Can't the augurers tell us a bit more?' asked Jamie.

'They are doing their best,' said the queen. 'But the dark magic surrounding Zora and Worfeus often clouds their visions. It is not always easy to see the present or the future as clearly as we would like.' Suddenly, the queen looked exhausted. Her eyes half closed, her lids fluttered and she seemed to slip into a faint. Her fairy-in-waiting rushed to her side.

'Her Majesty needs to rest,' said Lotus. 'Practising with the willow wand is exhausting. You should go now. We will send for you when there is news.'

Back at home, the children were anxious.

'I hope the queen will be all right,' said Luke.

'The fairies always look after her,' said Abigail.

'I hope so, because nothing is all right!' cried Jamie. 'Go back to normal, she said, go back to school. Seriously?'

'I don't think we have a choice,' said Jemima.

'It won't be for very long,' said Abigail. The others looked at her. 'Sorry, I don't know how long. I'd tell you if I did.'

'I almost wish the battle would happen right now, today, except that we need Queen Wanda to be in fighting form, and the Wandeleis' magic restored,' said Luke. 'This waiting around is so annoying.'

'And the more we think about it, the spookier it gets, doesn't it?' said Jemima.

The children tried not to talk about it again for the rest of the day. The ways of the magical world were different, and it was sometimes hard to accept. But no matter how long it took for the battle to come to them, they would have to wait as patiently as they could.

Chapter Three

BONES

Next morning, Teddy was in the house when he had an idea. He ran out through the cat flap and down the garden. He found Timber quickly. 'Greg has gone out and Gloria is planting herbs with Esther,' said Teddy. 'We could check out the cellar now.'

'Good idea,' said Timber. 'Esther should be able to keep Gloria distracted.'

'And we know where the key is,' said Teddy.

'We do,' said Timber. 'Come on.'

The children were in the fairy house waiting for Luke. Timber jumped on Jamie, pushing his muzzle into his chest. Teddy meowed loudly at Jemima.

'OK, what is it?' asked Jamie. Timber and Teddy bounded out the door. The three children followed quickly and Dougal scampered after them. Timber and Teddy waited by the back door for the children to catch up.

'Dougal,' barked Timber, 'we're going to take another look in the cellar. Wait here, and if Gloria or Esther come back into the house, bark like crazy.'

'OK,' said the spaniel. 'Be careful down there.'

'I'll keep you company,' said the Brigadier, trotting over. 'Two dogs barking are so much louder than one, except for Timber's big howl, of course.'

Timber went inside and sat in front of the kitchen cabinet where Greg had put the cellar key.

'Dad always puts stuff in here,' said Jamie, opening the drawer. He saw what he wanted. 'Yes!' He took the key and they hurried to the cellar. Timber and Teddy nearly knocked the children down with excitement as they clambered down the narrow staircase together.

'Wow, they're keen,' said Jamie.

'Maybe they know something,' said Jemima.

Timber barked his 'yes' bark as he leapt through the gap in the wall and ran to the corner where he had smelled the old bones. He and Teddy sniffed and pawed around a pile of rubble and rags in the corner, but without any light it was difficult for the children to see what they had found.

'I should have brought a torch,' said Jamie. 'I'll go and get one.'

'Hurry,' said Jemima. 'We'll be in trouble if Mum finds us here.'

Jamie ran upstairs and out to the shed in the yard. Dougal and the Brigadier were still sitting by the kitchen door.

'Jamie, did you forget to feed those two?' called Gloria, looking up from the herb garden as Jamie tore out of the house.

'Oh, um, I'll do that now,' said Jamie, over his shoulder on his way to the shed. He grabbed the torch and some dog food, plonked the food in the dogs' bowls and ran back inside.

The torch was a help but the cellar still had a thick fog of dust, making it difficult to see clearly. The children moved carefully, making sure not to disturb anything or make too much noise. They passed the portraits, and saw the boxes and a crate in one corner. There were mouldy curtains and moth-eaten rugs in another. A few chairs needing repair, a crate of empty bottles and another crate of jars were stacked along one wall. There was a faint but unpleasant smell coming from where Timber and Teddy were sniffing in the farthest corner. It was different from the musty old smell that was on everything else they had found.

The cat and dog turned, sat, and looked straight at the children.

'They *have* found something,' whispered Jemima.

Jamie, Jemima and Abigail walked slowly over. They stopped beside the pets and Jamie shone the light into the corner. Timber growled his warning growl. Teddy's fur stood on end. Moving the beam of light onto the lumpy pile, Jamie crouched down and carefully lifted the corner of an old sheet.

'Whoa!' he cried, dropping the cover. Both girls jumped, Timber barked, Teddy hissed.

'What is it?' whispered Jemima.

'I need to look again,' said Jamie. He lifted the sheet, more slowly this time. 'Bones,' he whispered. 'Definitely bones.'

'What kind?' asked Abigail.

'I don't know,' said Jamie. 'Small, chunky and . . . green . . . sort of.'

He pulled the sheet farther back to reveal not just two or three bones, but a scattered pile. The children

stared at them, while Timber trotted up and down, thinking. Teddy went in for another sniff.

'They look weird,' said Jamie.

'Tell me they're not human bones,' said Jemima.

'Short and thick,' said Abigail. 'They could belong to goblins.' She looked at the others. 'I might be able to tell if I touch them.'

'No!' cried Jemima. 'I mean, are you sure?'

'Is that another one of those knowing things you do?' asked Jamie.

'Sometimes it works,' said Abigail. She reached out her hand to touch the nearest bone, but pulled her hand away quickly. 'I think it was a goblin,' she said, 'a bad one.' She looked a little queasy.

'Luke found something in the puzzle about goblins,' said Jemima.

'He did,' said Jamie. 'And then we found the diary and that story about the two goblins. There has to be a connection.'

'The doorbell,' said Jemima suddenly. 'It's probably Luke, and if we don't answer it, Mum will, then she'll know we were down here.'

'Quick!' said Jamie.

Timber had already rushed ahead of them, having

heard Dougal and the Brigadier's barks. They all arrived upstairs, just in time to hear Gloria and Esther coming through to the kitchen. Jamie opened the front door. It was Luke, but Thaddeus had also arrived. He instantly saw that the children were up to something. First, they would have to deal with Gloria, then they could talk about it.

'They're definitely goblin bones,' said Thaddeus when they went down to take another look. 'I'll use a Concealment spell so Greg won't find them. And a Deterrent spell on the door so he might not feel like opening it.'

The children looked at him, unimpressed and anxious.

'It's the best I can do with my magic the way it is. And I'll have to tell Her Majesty. She'll decide what's to be done. Wait for me in the kitchen. It's best you're not here when I attempt these spells.'

Gloria was snoring softly in a chair, propped up with cushions after unknowingly drinking a sleeping draft. Esther had also prepared several mugs of hot chocolate while the children sat around the table. Timber and Teddy stayed beside them, wanting to hear what would be done about the bones.

'I hope at least one of those spells will hold,' said Thaddeus, sitting down beside Esther. 'It's difficult to get any spell to work these days.'

'Any idea when the Renewal charm will happen?' asked Jamie.

'We really need it to be soon,' added Luke.

'No word yet, I'm afraid,' said Thaddeus. 'Pearl is so tired, she's making mistakes restoring those two pages, and it takes a long time to redo such intricate work.'

The children were quiet.

'What is it?' asked Thaddeus. 'Did something else happen?'

Jamie explained what they had read in George's diary. 'You don't think George killed those two, do you?'

'Impossible,' said Thaddeus. 'As far as we know, George didn't have any magic, and goblins can only be killed with magic. No, something or someone magical killed them, or they killed each other.'

'If someone else was there, they might have killed them and then got away with the gold mentioned in the diary,' said Luke.

'We didn't find any gold down there,' said Jamie. 'But we didn't have enough time to look properly.'

'Leave the cellar for the moment,' said Esther. 'There could be remnants of goblin curses down there. Their magic is dark and powerful.'

'I did a quick sweep with my wand,' said Thaddeus, 'but it didn't reveal anything. We'll take another look, but only after I speak with the queen.'

'Who are these goblins?' said Jemima. 'We've never seen or heard of any.'

Thaddeus seemed reluctant to talk about goblins, but the children persisted.

'I found something about goblins in the puzzle,' said Luke. 'You remember, Professor? I think it was a warning, but it was very difficult to figure out.'

'I do remember,' said Thaddeus. 'Goblins haven't been seen around here for a long time, not since they finished mining all the gold in these parts. And goblins *always* follow the latest gold find; it's what they do. I'll ask Bushfire for an update on their whereabouts. The dwarfs used to work for the goblins, but they had a bad falling out. They still like to know their movements. Our dwarf friends are nearly finished rebuilding Hollow Hill by the way, and the queen hopes to return there soon. Anyone for more hot chocolate?'

Having managed to change the subject, Thaddeus smiled broadly, revealing his gold tooth. Although weakened like all the Wandeleis' magic, this time it managed to soothe everyone a little, and the professor didn't have to answer any more questions about goblins.

When the Allnutts had returned to their home in the village and Abigail had gone to bed, Thaddeus had a different conversation with Esther. 'This is deeply worrying,' he said. 'Bushfire and Jugjaw heard the goblins were on the move. After what I saw today, I think they might be on their way here, to Grindlewood.'

'To the scene of an old crime,' said Esther.

'Perhaps several crimes,' said Thaddeus. 'I hope to goodness old George wasn't hiding goblin gold, or worse still, that he didn't steal any! I must speak with the queen immediately.'

Chapter Four

WANDA'S WOES

The mounting troubles weighed heavily on Queen Wanda. Her enemies were gathering strength, and facing Worfeus and Zora together was a petrifying thought. She would have to consider using dark magic in the next encounter with the Worfagons, especially if the renewal of the Wandeleis' magic was delayed. Even then, she would need something extra, something special to deal with such force: the famous ancestral wand – the willow.

Wanda held it up to the moonlight. It was longer than the normal royal wand with a single streak of gold down one side – goblin gold. This wand had formidable power.

The willow, as it was known, had been made long

ago for Queen Cassandra as a coronation gift, crafted with special care, first by a Worfagon wand-maker, then imbued with magic by a goblin goldsmith. The goblin had owed the new queen a special favour and he included a touch of dark magic in the wand's core to give it extra strength. Later queens, including Queen Lyra, Wanda's predecessor, had found it too difficult to master. The wand was temperamental and responded only to a strong and confident owner after much practice. Until it was fully mastered, using it came at a price.

But there was no other plan, and no other way to defeat Zora and Worfeus together, a task the Wandelei queen knew she would have to perform alone, according to *The Book of Prophecies.*

Wanda's decision to use the willow worried her professors. Only the wand's first owner, Queen Cassandra, had mastered it, and there was no guarantee that Queen Wanda would master it too. The magical element inside the wand was ageing her, and already she looked older than her years. She was often tired and cranky, and more recently she was prone to bouts of fainting, but the professors could only look on in dismay.

Thaddeus had a number of troubling issues to discuss with the queen and the professors. When he arrived, he got straight to the point. 'Is there any more news about the goblins?'

'Worryingly, no,' said Sparks. 'We don't know what they're up to.'

Thaddeus explained about the discovery in the cellar. 'Bones, Your Majesty. I saw them myself and I am certain they belong to two goblins.'

'Merlin's beard!' cried Flint.

'Two?' cried Sparks. 'You don't think George –'

'Calm down, gentlemen,' said the queen crossly.

'They probably killed each other,' said Pendrick.

'That's what I thought,' said Thaddeus, 'but there may have been a third goblin involved, who escaped.'

'I'm surprised we didn't hear about this before now,' said Wanda. 'Although goblins are never mentioned in *The Book of Prophecies*; they are considered *un*worthy.'

'Goblins abandon their dead,' said Sparks. 'They're not a lovable lot.'

'But they would return for gold,' said Flint. 'If that's what they were after, others will follow.'

'I did a sweep-search with my wand but found nothing,' said Thaddeus. 'I also used a couple of spells to hide the find, though I'm not sure they will hold. You know what our magic is like at the moment.'

'It's rubbish,' muttered Sparks.

'Indeed,' said Pendrick. 'And the goblins don't have the same renewal problems as we do.'

'Despite our current difficulties, that is all we can do to conceal those bones for the moment,' said the queen. 'What about the portal in the garden? Timber was concerned that it needed more protection too.'

'I tried a few Protection charms, Your Majesty,' said Sparks. 'So did Professor Pendrick, but our magic is so unstable.'

'Yes, and?'

'The well is better protected now,' said Sparks, 'but not quite how we intended.'

The queen looked impatient, so Pendrick explained: 'The well is filled with stones and covered in barbed wire, Your Majesty. Whether it can operate as a portal or not is uncertain, though I fear it may be possible.'

'Anyone who uses it will end up in the barbed wire,' said Sparks, trying to sound optimistic.

'I don't think barbed wire will stop the Worfagons!' cried the queen. 'And certainly not Zora or Worfeus.'

After an awkward silence, Thaddeus tried to steer the conversation to other news and updates. 'The magical learning lessons with the children are continuing.'

'Good,' said the queen.

'The wizards said that the boys are doing very well at fencing and archery,' added Pendrick.

'And you know how hard Luke has worked on our puzzle,' said Thaddeus. 'We really are doing all we can.'

'It's a pity we haven't finished it,' said Wanda. 'We may have missed some clue about the orb, how to approach it, use it, what kind of magic protects it, and how to stop it falling into our enemies' hands.'

Thaddeus nodded, wondering if he could say anything that would cheer the queen. 'The fairies are very pleased with the girls' spells classes. Jemima is advancing quicker than expected, for a non-witch of course.'

'Yes,' said the queen. 'But Elva tells me Abigail's heart is not in it. What is the matter?'

'Unlike yourself and your niece, Your Majesty, most witches and wizards excel in only one area of magic,' said Pendrick. 'Abigail has always shown talent for knowing, as you did at her age, but she is also very gifted at art and restoration.'

'She loves it,' said Thaddeus.

'It must be difficult to concentrate on what you're really good at *and* try to learn your spells,' said Pendrick.

'Perhaps she should spend some time helping Pearl,' muttered Thaddeus, though the idea worried him.

'As for Jemima,' continued Pendrick, 'she has *inherited* a touch of goblin magic from her great-great-aunt, which explains how she is learning so quickly. It must be said that as a non-witch she doesn't have any other magical abilities and therefore has fewer distractions.'

'We should keep a close eye on her,' said Flint, 'and watch how her magic develops.'

'I doubt if Krool gave much magic to Jemima's ancestor,' said Thaddeus. 'But you're right, Flint, we should be wary. It is Jemima's pure heart and unshakable belief that makes her magic appear so natural. Quite extraordinary.'

Wanda sighed. 'Very well, gentlemen, keep me updated. Despite the news of the goblin bones, our most urgent issue is still the restoration of *The Book of Darkness*, and the renewal of our magic. But I agree that Pearl needs help. I will speak with her now.' The queen nodded to Lotus who went off to fetch Pearl.

A few minutes later, the two fairies joined the queen and the professors. Pearl looked distressed and weary.

'How is the restoration coming along?' asked the queen.

'Your Majesty, I am doing my best,' said Pearl, 'but it is difficult work, and the more I hurry, the more mistakes I make.' She burst into tears.

'I understand, dear, but you are our most skilled restorer, and this task is so important to us,' said the queen. 'Who is helping you?'

'Elva and Spira were with me at the start,' said Pearl, wiping her eyes, 'but as the work became more difficult, their hands were shaking too much and they couldn't continue. I am doing the last few pieces alone, but they are the most intricate. One mistake now and the whole page must be redone.'

The queen took a sharp breath. Redoing an entire page could take weeks, and that could have disastrous consequences. 'What about Abigail?' she asked. 'My niece has been working on *The Book of Enchantments* all by herself. You admired her work. Do you think she would be able to help you?'

'She is very talented, Your Majesty,' said Pearl, 'but *The Book of Darkness* is different from other books. It's as if the book itself is willing you to fail, and with every step you become weaker, more tired, more fearful and then the trembling starts.' Pearl held up her right hand; it was red-raw and shaking. Lotus brought her some Calming lemonade.

'That settles it,' said the queen. 'Abigail must help you, starting tomorrow. Lotus will look after you this evening, Pearl. Go now, get some rest while the inks are drying.'

The fairies departed and Wanda retired to her private chamber. The professors looked worried, Sparks in particular.

'I know what you're thinking,' said Thaddeus. 'But practising with the willow is bound to make the queen cross.'

'I fear it may darken her mood permanently,' said Sparks.

'It may affect her decision-making too,' added Flint.

They were quiet for a moment, reflecting on their woes.

'It's a lot to ask of Abigail, but I do think it's the right decision,' said Pendrick.

'Oh, yes, I agree,' said Sparks. 'I've heard she is very skilled, but that's not what worries me most.'

Pendrick's face blanched. 'Do you think Her Majesty is considering an *attack*?'

'Queen Lyra almost did, once,' said Sparks. 'Just after she was cursed to grow like a tree. And Queen Wanda is pushing herself very hard. I worry she will collapse or that she will make a grave error of judgement.'

'We would be sent to the magical wilderness if we broke that rule again,' cried Pendrick. 'She wouldn't. She couldn't!'

'She might,' said Sparks.

'Lotus said she was talking in her sleep,' said Flint.

'She's worried, that's all. She has a lot to think about,' said Thaddeus. 'Queen Wanda would never break the Ancients' rule, not after Queen Cassandra's disastrous war.'

'I hope you're right,' said Sparks.

The professors returned to their duties, more disturbed than ever.

The goblins weren't just gathering and grumbling as the dwarfs had reported. They were up to no good.

'I was surprised Audmund had the nerve to ask us to copy the gold and silver keys,' said the goblin known as Claw.

'Whatever he's up to, he must believe it was worth the risk,' said Krag, the goblin king. 'What information did you pry from him?'

'He said the Grindles were back in the big house,' said Claw, 'and we all know that a stash of gold went missing in Grindlewood when old George lived there.'

'But we don't know that George took it,' said an older goblin.

'Krool disappeared around that time, didn't he?' said the goblin named Dregs.

'So what?' said Claw.

'George wasn't a bad sort,' said the older one, ignoring the other two. 'Kept to himself, worked hard, looked after his silly sister-in-law. Krool, on the other hand, was a trouble-maker.'

'Who cares?' cried another. 'That old Grindle is dead, but his family might know where our gold is. It could be somewhere in that house.'

'What do you say, Krag?' asked Dregs. 'If our gold was stolen, can't we steal it back?'

The others cheered their agreement.

'Of course we can,' said Krag. More cheering. 'But something bigger is going on, I can feel it. And why does Audmund want to meet us again? What does he want this time?'

'More keys?' suggested one.

Krag sneered at him and the goblin fell silent.

'Maybe he wants a cut of our gold once we get it back?' offered another.

He received a sneer too.

'Like I said,' said Krag. 'We need to know what's *really* going on. Claw, meet Audmund and find out what he wants. I think he's keeping secrets, especially from his Worfagon friends, and that means he's up to something sneaky. If it sounds like it's worth our while, bring him to see me.'

Claw grunted and nodded to a small group who followed him out of the chamber.

'I'll be meeting Worfeus soon too,' said Krag. 'He's back from Warlock Hell, and he says he has an interesting proposition.'

Chapter Five

UNEASY ALLIES

Inside Mord Manor, Zora was guzzling potions to speed up her recovery. Her progress had come to a sudden halt after she used the Destroyer spell on Hollow Hill. Though furious with her brother for banishing her to the Outer Oblivion, so far, Zora had avoided a confrontation. There had been bickering and arguments, but she could not risk a duel with Worfeus while she was still in a weakened state. Her revenge would have to be carefully timed and calculated.

Lord Vargon's workload was taking a heavy toll on the old tutor. His spider-work and poison-brewing were tiring enough, but trying to control Zora was really exhausting him. Vargon knew he would have to come up with a plan for dealing with Worfeus soon too. The twins would never agree to rule together, but he knew which one he favoured.

Once Zora was strong again, they could return to Vargon's plan and focus their attention on finding the orb, defeating the enemy and then finally crowning Zora the new queen of Grindlewood. The orb was essential to ensuring their success. In the meantime everyone had to put up with each other's annoying habits.

Audmund was keeping out of everyone's way, avoiding arguments and difficult questions. He had expected Worfeus to deal with Zora immediately, but it was clear that the warlock had a different plan for his twin sister. 'Perhaps he's afraid of what this orb can do,' he thought. 'He might even need his sister's power as well as his own to control it, if, as everyone expects, the orb proves to be dangerous. The fool! Just like those augurers, terrified out of their wits at any mention of the orb. Well, let them all worry while I sneak off with the orb behind their backs. Ha!'

Discussions in the parlour after supper were always difficult. It was the one time of the day that Vargon insisted they get together and talk about their plans, or rather *his* plan. Everyone turned up eventually, if only to make sure they didn't miss something.

'I see that eagle is still around,' said Vargon. 'He could be a spy, Zora. How can you be sure he isn't loyal to those children and Timber?'

'We already agreed that he might be useful,' said Zora. 'And he will look lovely at my coronation. Anyway, I don't believe he is fond of the Grindles at all. How could he be?'

'Don't tell me those do-gooders from the garden are still causing trouble,' said Worfeus.

'They gave *you* plenty of trouble in the past,' said Vargon.

Worfeus gave him such a terrifying glare, Vargon had a sudden coughing fit. Worfeus had always detested Lord Vargon, the royal tutor who favoured his sister over him. He secretly wanted to kill him, but he was smart enough to realise that if Vargon wanted this orb so badly, it must be worth having. Worfeus would play along with Vargon's plans, suspecting that the crafty old tutor hadn't told anyone the whole story. For now, everyone was useful, even Vargon.

'His Lordship is right about one thing, Zora,' said Worfeus. 'You cannot use the Destroyer spell, or not only will you damage yourself but you might end up destroying the orb before we even find it.'

'I want to destroy that queen and everything she owns!' cried Zora.

'And you will,' said Worfeus. 'Just not the orb, if you don't mind.'

'Those do-gooders are called the Grindlewood Army now,' said Audmund.

'The what?' cried Worfeus. He turned to his sister. 'Why didn't you destroy *them* instead of Hollow Hill?'

Zora glared at him. 'Because I am *a queen*, and I will fight Queen Wanda, not some lowly collection of nobodies.'

'To be fair, they have been surprisingly brave,' said Audmund.

'Really!' said Vargon crossly. 'Have you all forgotten the plan, *my* plan?'

'They are in the prophecy too,' said Audmund, ignoring Vargon. 'I heard the augurers mumbling about them many times.'

'Well, we won't be caught out again,' said Worfeus.

'Nothing will stand in our way,' said Zora. 'The orb will be kept in our new kingdom, once we take possession of it, and we will reign supreme just like our father wished. Isn't that right, brother – together?' She attempted a smile.

'Eh, yes, of course, together,' replied Worfeus, followed by one of his own equally insincere smiles. 'There will be plenty of power to share once we have the orb.'

'Did you hear anything about the orb in Warlock Hell?' asked Audmund. 'What sort of power it holds, perhaps? Or how we might unlock it?' Everyone glared at him. None of them liked to be reminded of how little they actually knew about the orb.

Worfeus did not answer.

'We do *not* know,' said Vargon. 'Oscar was very clever but he told no one what he put in the orb, nor how his wife made it. They are the best-kept secrets in the magical world.'

'It doesn't matter what kind of power it holds,' said Zora. 'We'll find out soon enough. Anyway, power –'

'– is power,' finished Worfeus. 'And we will master it.'

Vargon cast a worried glance in Audmund's direction.

Zora retired to her bedroom to take her Youth serum at precisely nine o'clock. Vargon went to his study to brew some more of his lumpy brown potion.

Audmund and Worfeus were alone for a few minutes.

'Why do you keep bringing up those children and that dog?' asked Worfeus.

'Because they caused you so much trouble before,' said Audmund, 'and I would prefer if we didn't have a repeat performance.'

'Do you think I need reminding?' Worfeus looked like he was suddenly possessed by thunder.

'Probably not,' said Audmund, as calmly as he could. 'But before you threaten me, please remember that I brought you back from hell. You owe me a great debt.'

'Perhaps,' said Worfeus, 'though it depends on how things turn out.'

'If we get the orb, things will turn out very well,' said Audmund.

Worfeus studied Audmund for a minute, knowing he wouldn't be able to tolerate him for much longer either. He decided to change the subject. 'I will be leaving in the morning to round up my old warriors. I expect you to keep an eye and an ear on Zora and Vargon. They're far too cosy for my liking, despite their recent disagreements. Vargon will try to turn her against me, so a close bond between them doesn't bode well for either of us.'

'Understood,' said Audmund. 'You've spent most of the summer visiting your old haunts gathering this great army of yours. I hope it'll be a better army than the last lazy lot. How long will you be?'

'A few days should finalise everything,' said Worfeus. 'It's important I choose the most loyal warlocks. I want this battle to put an end to those Wandeleis once and for all. I intend to rule a powerful Grindlewood Realm, that will outshine every kingdom in history.' Worfeus bent low and put his face right in to Audmund's. 'Don't let things get out of hand while I'm away.' He left the room.

Later, alone in his study, Audmund went over his own plan.

'Worfeus, Zora and Vargon,' he thought. 'Underneath, they hate and distrust one another, but that should be to my advantage.' He chuckled to himself until a feeling of dread crept up his spine. He had arranged another meeting with the goblins. Involving them was risky, but if everything worked out as he planned, Zora and Worfeus would kill each other, perhaps Wanda and Vargon too. He would bribe the goblins, blame the Grindles for the loss of the goblins' gold, just to add to the confusion, and then escape with the orb.

He was surprised by a knock on the door. It was Vargon.

'I said I'd pay you a visit sometime,' he said, pushing past. 'We need to talk about those twins.'

Vargon thought that a back-up plan might be wise.

'It's always good to be prepared,' said Audmund. 'Zora and Worfeus are headstrong as well as powerful. We should watch our step.'

'We need to do more than that,' said Vargon. 'We must not be fooled into thinking that our powers can match theirs. They can't. Now show me what you've been up to.'

'I beg your pardon?' said Audmund, his nerves suddenly tingling.

'I know you've been making poisons,' said Vargon. 'So have I, and there's no point in the two of us making the same brews when we could be making different ones. Show me what you've got so we can get organised.'

Audmund went over to a tall cabinet, unlocked the doors and opened them wide. The shelves were packed with a range of potions and poisons in jars, bottles and vials.

'You have been busy,' said Vargon. 'So, we both secretly fear the same thing – one or both of those two getting out of control. I'm glad that idiot Valerius Vole didn't survive the return from Warlock Hell too.'

'Yes, Valerius is one problem we don't have to worry about,' said Audmund. 'I'll start collecting the rest of the ingredients, shall I?'

'Do that,' said Vargon, 'and I'll extract more venom from the spiders. Keep this between us, Audmund. Those two could join forces against us, despite their chequered past. If they spot a weakness or think they can manage without us, we're in big trouble. I'm not sure they know the depths of their own power yet, and it's better that way, trust me. I've known them a long time.'

Audmund flinched at the thought. Together Zora and Worfeus would be a formidable force. He had simply assumed they would be at each other's throats, though there was still time for that. 'Worfeus is visiting the old dimensions one last time to round up more warriors,' he said. 'That should keep him out of our way for a few days.'

'I've suggested to Zora that she chooses a new wardrobe for the big showdown,' said Vargon. 'That'll keep her busy.'

'Will you be enhancing the hawks and bats?' asked Audmund.

'Most certainly,' said Vargon, 'and I have something for that knuckle-headed dwarf-troll too.'

'Leave him till last, will you?' Audmund didn't like anyone meddling with his pet dwarf-troll, Grizzle.

'I suppose we've enough to do for now,' said Vargon. He turned at the door, nodded briefly and left.

It was a strange turn of events for Lord Vargon to want Audmund as an ally against Zora and Worfeus. But Audmund still didn't trust him. He didn't trust anyone. Nonetheless, he thought about their conversation long into the night.

❧

Worfeus paid a visit to his sister before he left. He needed to stay on her good side for as long as possible in case he needed her, before he sent her back to the Outer Oblivion. He swept into Zora's room.

'Hello, sister dear. I must say that Youth serum is giving spectacular results. You look positively radiant!'

'What? Oh, yes, I am beautiful again,' said Zora, looking in her wall of mirrors. Then she turned quickly to face him. 'Worfeus! We have to talk about that Banishment spell. Why, I can't even remember exactly how long I was locked up in that horrid cube, but, how dare you! I mean, how could you? I, I . . .'

'There you are,' interrupted Worfeus. 'It's already a fading memory, and you're looking lovelier than ever. Sit down, Zora. You'll be delighted with what I have to tell you.'

The flattery took Zora by surprise, even though she was furious.

'I know what I did was dreadful,' Worfeus continued, 'but we were young and foolish, and now that I'm back, I can be very useful. No one has the kind of power I have, power that only comes from the deepest, darkest reaches of hell. I have powers that no one has ever seen before, I'm sure of it. I can feel it.'

'Feel it? How do you know?' asked Zora.

'Why, eh, everyone in hell told me,' said Worfeus. 'You'll see for yourself soon, in the battle.'

'I don't believe anyone could be more powerful than me, once I am fully well again,' said Zora. 'But I look forward to your demonstration.'

'Thank you,' said Worfeus. 'Now listen. We have an opportunity to defeat all our enemies once and for all. All those who have wronged us, annoyed us, irritated us.'

'I know,' said Zora.

'Of course,' said Worfeus. 'We will be the undisputed king and queen of, eh, Worfagonia, is it? I rather like the name Grindlewood Realm, myself.'

'Worfagonia,' said Zora proudly, gazing into the distance as she imagined herself crowned queen.

'Fine,' said Worfeus. 'First, we must be united in our plan – *our* plan, Zora – to get the orb.'

'We still don't know where it is, as everyone keeps reminding me.'

'A minor detail,' said Worfeus. 'I'm sure that sneaky augurer and that conniving tutor know more than they're letting on.'

'You think so?' said Zora. 'Is Vargon conniving?'

'Probably,' said Worfeus. 'But we won't be needing either of them for much longer.'

'Not even to find the orb?'

'I'm sure it's in that garden,' said Worfeus. 'Everything revolves around Grindlewood and that wretched dog.'

'You have a point,' said Zora.

'Vargon and Audmund are not royals. They don't deserve to share what is rightfully ours – power and authority to rule far and wide, just as Father would have wanted. The power of the orb will ensure it, and we don't want Vargon or Audmund getting in the way, now do we?'

Zora stared at him. 'Absolutely not.'

'You remember my goblin friends?'

Zora nodded with a scowl.

'Don't worry, I know they smell, but you can leave them to me. I will convince them to join us, cause a few diversions, tactics, Zora, battle plans, that sort of thing. They'll do whatever I ask.'

'You think so?' Zora had a hint of a sneer in her voice.

But Worfeus didn't notice the sneer. It was his turn to think of all the adoration he would receive as the newly crowned king. That would certainly impress the goblins. Perhaps they would give him a haul of gold as a coronation gift. Maybe they would make him an elaborate gold crown too.

'I suppose they might be useful for the dirty work,' said Zora.

'Exactly,' said Worfeus. 'We needn't be involved in all that messy fighting. Royalty should oversee what the minions are doing, and then arrive for the final moment of glory – and take the prize – the orb, which will help us create the greatest kingdom in history.'

They finished their conversation in what sounded like agreement, but they were both smart enough to fear the other's power, and wonder about each other's true intentions.

Chapter Six

PROBLEMS

The golden eagle had two big problems. He hadn't been able to unravel the symbols on his last piece of parchment; and he knew that everyone in Mord Manor was suspicious of him. 'This is beyond disappointing!' he cried. There was no option now but to ask for help, something he hated doing.

Bodric Buzzard wasn't exactly a friend – sometimes he was more like an enemy – but the two birds tolerated each other once they could do each other a favour now and then. The eagle surprised the buzzard as he arrived through the portal at the back of Grindlewood Forest.

'Argh! Gildevard, you startled me!' cried Bodric.

'Feeling a bit nervous, Bodric?' said the eagle. 'I thought you would be chuffed with yourself. Now that Ripley has scarpered, you must be Zora's top spy.'

'Yes, I am, of course I am,' said Bodric, 'and good riddance to that horrid squirrel. What do you want?'

'A favour,' said the eagle, as coolly as possible.

'What?' cried the buzzard. 'After all the insults and sneers? Not likely.'

'I have another piece of parchment,' said the eagle. 'I think it could be the one that contains the location of the orb. Sure you don't want to take a little peek?'

Bodric's eyes widened with interest, then narrowed again as he considered what it was worth to the eagle. 'What do I get for this privilege?'

'Knowing what's on the parchment is reward enough, and a privilege only you and I will have,' said the eagle. 'Then it will be you who owes me, Bodric, not the other way around.'

'That's debatable,' said the buzzard. 'What's to stop me telling Zora?'

'You might like to think on that,' said Gildevard.

Bodric eyed him, unsure of what he meant.

'Once Zora gets the orb, she won't need us any more,' said the eagle. 'Everyone is after it, so time is running out. I have the parchment with me. Will you take a look or not?'

'If I refuse?' asked Bodric.

'I'll tell Zora you were keeping something important from her,' said Gildevard. 'She listens to me more than you realise.'

Bodric paced up and down, fluffing his feathers, his head tucked low as he thought about it. 'How can you be sure the location is on that little piece of parchment, *and* that it's the right location? Zora'll be furious if the information is wrong.'

'I've deciphered enough around the edges of the piece to know that –'

'Around the edges! You are losing your touch,' said Bodric. 'Give it here, and make sure I get all the credit for this.'

Gildevard showed him the parchment, which he had gripped in one of his talons.

'Where did you get it?' asked Bodric as he opened it out.

'I pick up interesting things on my travels,' said Gildevard.

The buzzard studied the symbols in silence. It wasn't as easy as the other piece the eagle had shown him, but he wasn't going to admit that. As always, he would give away as little as possible.

Talk of the orb came up at every meeting in the garden. At first, the pets had been divided about what should be done about it. As the weeks went by, most were glad that it hadn't been brought into their garden. After all, the children wore the four keys around their necks, they knew how to unlock the puzzles and codes to each door in the maze, and only Timber's paw could open the fifth lock, the one that revealed Othelia's Orb. Surely it was safe where it was? That night, however, Timber told them the time had come to move it.

'How will we explain that to the children?' asked Teddy.

'When we go to the forest for our next walk, we'll lead them straight to the lair,' said Timber. 'I think they'll take the hint.'

'We'll have to be careful we're not spotted,' said Dougal.

'Very careful,' said Timber. 'Oberon, blackbirds, sparrows and woodpigeons: you will scout along the route to make sure it is clear before we leave and while we are on the walk.' The birds tooted and twittered agreement. 'Foxes, rabbits: you will run either side of us, but not too close. I need you to cover as wide an area as possible.'

'To check for spies,' said Eldric.

Timber nodded.

'What about us?' asked Cindy, sounding a bit put out. Teddy was looking a bit glum too.

'I'll need you, Cindy and Teddy, to guard the garden,' said Timber. 'Sylvie, the Brigadier, the heron and the swans too.'

'Suddenly, there doesn't seem to be enough of us,' said the hedgehog. 'Am I to stay here as well?'

'Yes, Norville, and the robins too,' said Timber. 'Teddy, you'll be in charge.'

Teddy looked pleased again, and Cindy calmed down. The cats were never taken for a walk like the dogs, and sometimes they felt left out of the action.

'Once we're in the lair,' continued Timber, 'Trigger

and Dougal will stand guard, while the foxes and rabbits patrol nearby. The birds will spread out through the trees.'

'Where will we put the orb once we get it?' asked Teddy.

'The only place I can think of is in the pond,' said Timber.

'That would be very clever, except that the pond usually freezes during winter,' said Eldric.

'I know,' said Timber, 'but I can't think of anywhere else it will fit, won't be broken and won't be seen. It might be a good thing if the pond freezes and no one can get it.'

'Maybe the children will have another idea,' said Sylvie.

'Perhaps they could take the orb to the Eastern Woods,' said Oberon.

'I thought of that,' said Timber. 'But the queen is worried about spies.'

'More spies?' cried Norville. 'In that magical place?'

'She's not sure,' said Timber. 'But it means we'll probably have to keep the orb here in the garden, at least for now.'

'Then the fight will come to us this time,' said Dougal.

'I know and I hate the thought of it,' said Timber. 'Everyone will be after the orb.'

The next day, the children were in the yard getting the dog leashes, while all the animals and birds not on patrol gathered at the fairy house. Timber and Dougal sat at the front of the group and barked loudly as the children headed towards them.

'This sounds urgent,' said Jamie.

'They look so serious,' said Jemima.

The pets sat motionless, eyes fixed on the children. As they came closer, Timber and Dougal hopped up and ran to the gap in the hedge. They stood there, waiting, excited and keen to go.

'Off you go, Trigger,' said Luke. 'Join your pals.' Having just arrived, Luke let Trigger off his leash and he bounded after the others. The dogs ran through the hedge and into the neighbouring field. Oberon flew overhead with some of the birds to scout ahead.

'Looks like we're going to the forest again,' said Jemima.

'With a scouting party,' said Luke, looking up.

'The rabbits and foxes too,' said Abigail. The three

foxes and five rabbits dashed out of the garden after them. Dozens more rabbits joined them and they scurried around the field and on into the forest, just as Timber had instructed.

When the children caught up with the dogs, they found all three sitting at the entrance to Worfeus' old lair. Oberon was perched just above them on a branch.

Suddenly, there was a haunting screech overhead. The golden eagle circled then swooped down and perched beside the snowy owl. Oberon gave him a cross look.

Timber was also annoyed. Their plan to move the orb was now scuppered.

The children sensed the unease and none of them went near the lair. They sat down on a fallen tree trunk and watched the animals and birds for a few moments. It was clear they were talking about something, and the conversation was tense.

'Hello, Gildevard,' said Timber. 'We didn't expect to see you.'

'I thought you'd like to know that Bodric is nosing around,' said the eagle.

'Thanks for the warning,' said Timber. 'Where did you see him?'

‘At the far end of the forest,’ said the eagle. ‘I chased him off but he could still be sneaking around. He normally returns to the manor just before dark.’

‘We’re on a walk,’ said Timber. ‘Are you coming to the garden today?’

‘No, perhaps another time.’ The eagle flew off.

‘Well, I never!’ cried the owl.

‘That was abrupt,’ said Dougal. ‘Should we believe him?’

‘Sounded a bit suspicious to me,’ said Trigger. ‘Maybe it was the eagle who was nosing around.’

‘We can’t let Bodric or Gildevard near the orb,’ said Timber. ‘We’ll have to come back tomorrow.’

‘Perhaps not in the daytime,’ said Oberon. ‘Gildevard said Bodric returns to the manor before dark. I think he’s right about that. I heard Bodric is afraid to be on his own in the dark.’

‘It might be better to move the orb at night anyway,’ said Timber. He woofed at Jamie and nuzzled at the leash.

‘Want to go home?’ asked Jamie. Timber barked his ‘yes’ bark.

‘They weren’t very happy to see the eagle,’ said Luke. ‘I wonder what that was about?’

'Timber wanted us to go into the lair, didn't he?' said Jemima.

'But not while the eagle's around,' said Jamie.

'If they don't trust him, we shouldn't either,' said Abigail.

'Timber wants us to move the orb. I'm sure of it,' said Jamie.

Timber barked his 'yes' bark again.

'We need to think of somewhere we can hide it,' said Jamie. 'Come on, we'll talk in the fairy house.'

Gildevard caught up with the buzzard again. He was chewing a few nuts near the portal at the end of the forest. 'Still here, Bodric?'

'I thought you might like some company in Worfeus' lair.'

'You thought wrong,' said the eagle. 'But I think you wanted to see if the orb was really there, and if it was, would the children move it somewhere else. I know you better than you think.'

'Tut, tut, Gildevard, you wouldn't have known where to look if I hadn't helped you,' said Bodric. 'And yes, I have to check my information before telling Zora anything. Like I said before, she doesn't like mistakes.'

'It's getting late. Won't Zora be looking for you?'

'She would use the Mind-meld to call me if it was urgent,' said Bodric.

'Perhaps she's saving her energy.'

Whether that was true or not, it was certainly possible, and it annoyed the buzzard when the eagle was right. 'Let me know if you see the orb, won't you?' said Bodric, and he popped through the portal.

Gildevard headed back to the lair, ducking through the trees to make sure he wasn't spotted. The last thing he wanted to do was show Bodric the piece of parchment, but he couldn't change that now. If only he had watched and waited, he might have figured out that the children and Timber already knew the location of the orb. Now Zora would hear about it as well. 'Perhaps she won't say anything just yet,' thought the eagle. 'She won't want anyone else to know until she has regained all her strength.'

Looking around to make sure he wasn't seen, Gildevard entered the lair. He saw the stone at the back, and his sharp eyes quickly picked out the lock carved amongst the symbols. It needed a special key, and no doubt beyond that door there were more obstacles, and magic too. He would not be able to reach the orb on his own, but he could wait for the moment when someone else did. And that would happen soon.

❧

The children had just sat down in the fairy house when the butterflies arrived with a worrying message.

If evil takes the orb, all will be lost,
The worthy must get to it first –
Find all the spies, keep the orb safe,
or all in this land will be cursed!

'No more delays,' said Jamie. 'We have to go tonight.'

'In the dark?' said Jemima.

'We have torches,' said Jamie, 'and it's pitch dark in the maze anyway.'

'What about Dad?' said Jemima. 'He's out all day, but he hardly sleeps when he comes home. He spends most of the night reading George's papers.'

'We could try a Sleeping spell,' said Abigail.

'Have you learned one yet?' said Luke.

'Em, no,' said Abigail. 'But they're in my *Book of Spells.* They don't look too difficult.'

The others weren't too keen. Abigail blushed. Everyone knew that her spell lessons hadn't advanced any further than Jemima's, though they should have.

'A spell like that might be tricky,' said Jemima thoughtfully.

'Right,' said Jamie. 'Once we take the orb out of the maze, where will we put it?'

'Is there any way we could get an Invisibility chest?' said Jemima.

'That's still the best idea,' said Luke.

'No,' said Abigail. 'Granddad hasn't had time to make a new one.'

'We're not getting very far, are we?' said Jamie.

'If you don't like the spell idea, we could try a Sleeping potion,' said Abigail. 'Aunt Tamara is an expert. I could take a look at her potions notebook.'

'Now, that's a good idea!' said Jamie.

Everyone agreed.

'We'll need scouts to keep a lookout when we move the orb,' said Luke.

Timber nosed the door open and trotted inside. He had been listening near the door and keeping an eye on the well at the same time. When he heard the mention of scouts he came in, woofing softly.

'I think our scouting parties are ready,' said Jamie. He gave Timber a hug.

'That leaves the hiding place,' said Luke. 'Maybe it would fit in here?' He looked at the old hiding place they had under the floorboards. It was too long and narrow. 'Never mind, that won't work.'

'We could take it into the house,' said Jemima.

'What if Mum and Dad find it?' said Jamie. 'No, not the house, and the barn won't do either. Dad's always in and out of there.'

'What about the pond?' said Luke.

Timber growled his interested growl, a long, low, rolling one.

'The scroll was safe there,' said Jemima, 'but the orb is more awkward.'

'I wonder will the orb want to move,' said Abigail. The others looked at her for an explanation. 'It must be protected by magic, even when it leaves the Pyramid Tomb. We should be careful. We don't know what powers it might have. Maybe it can move, or fly, or even disappear.'

No one had thought of that.

‘OK,’ said Jamie after a moment’s thought. ‘Once we sort out Mum and Dad, we get the orb and we put it in the pond, unless we think of somewhere better, and unless the orb has some other idea. Agreed?’

The children’s plan was one Sleeping potion away from ready.

Chapter Seven

THE TOMB

Bodric had to be careful what he told Zora. But he was trying to be too clever and ended up rambling. 'The parchment was faded and tatty, Your Redness. I deciphered everything that was still visible.'

Zora stood gazing out the window and didn't reply.

'I think the children want to move the orb,' the buzzard continued more eagerly. 'I heard them talking about it, but they haven't thought of a suitable place to hide it.'

'So, you don't know where it is or where it will be. Is that all?' said Zora, turning abruptly.

'Well, I, eh, I had two near escapes just trying to find out that much,' said Bodric meekly.

'Next time, make sure you are certain before you

come waffling to me!' Zora roared at him. 'Do not waste my time, Bodric.'

'Yes, Your Redness.' Foolishly, Bodric tried one more time. 'The eagle may decide to help the Grindlewood Army,' he said. 'If he does, the orb will fall into Wanda's hands. What do you want me to do now, Your Redness?'

'Keep an eye on them like you're supposed to,' she snapped. 'What the eagle does is no concern of yours. I am confident he will deliver the orb. Even if you have a keen sense of smell, his eyes and ears are sharper than yours.'

'But how could he move an orb, Your Redness? He is a bird, just like me.'

'He is a golden eagle and you are a mere buzzard,' said Zora. 'Gildevard will tell us when those children get the orb, where they put it, and then I will send Audmund to fetch it. Now get out, you idiot! I don't have to explain myself to you.'

Bodric shuffled off, frustrated and miserable.

It was a little after midnight. The children peeped out of their bedrooms to see what was happening.

'No sign,' whispered Jemima. 'Maybe they fell asleep on the couch.'

'How long does a Sleeping potion take to work?' asked Jamie.

'I don't know,' said Abigail. 'It depends on so many things.'

'What?' cried Luke. 'We could be waiting for hours.'

'Shh,' said Jamie. 'If they are getting sleepy, we don't want to wake them up again.'

'I think I hear Mum coming,' said Jemima.

Sure enough, Gloria was heading upstairs, yawning. Jamie listened at the bedroom door to hear whether she had actually gone to bed. Once he heard her snoring softly, he ran back to his own bedroom to report to the others.

'She's asleep,' he said. 'Well done, Abi. Now we need Dad to do the same.'

Greg stayed downstairs, however, reading George's papers for another hour. As the children grew impatient, Jemima put on her pyjamas and crept downstairs, pretending to fetch a glass of water. But she needn't have bothered. Her father was finally asleep in an armchair. Jemima noticed lipstick on two mugs sitting on the side table.

'Mum must have drunk a double dose,' she said to the others when she went back upstairs. 'I saw her lipstick on both mugs.'

'That's why she conked out like that,' said Jamie.

'Then your dad might only have had half a dose, or maybe none at all,' said Luke. 'He could wake up any minute.'

'We can't wait any longer,' said Jamie. 'We'll just have to be really quiet.'

Abigail nudged Jemima. 'We should take the last three gems,' she said. 'I've a bad feeling about that Pyramid Tomb.'

'Good idea,' said Jemima. 'I'll get the gems when I change my clothes. Back in a minute.'

The children moved very carefully past the study. Greg was still asleep, snoring now. They grabbed their hats, coats, scarves, gloves and torches. Jamie also pulled his rucksack and a small blanket out of the cupboard.

'For the orb,' he whispered.

The others nodded.

Outside, Timber checked that the animals and birds were in their correct groups. They set off as arranged through the trees, up in the sky and spread out across the ground. Teddy took charge in the garden, keeping watch by the well with Cindy. Timber, Dougal, Trigger and Oberon waited by the gap in the hedge for the children.

There was no moon that night. Oberon flew a little ahead, circling back occasionally, while the dogs stayed close to the children. They crossed the field and entered the forest, stopping outside the lair. They took out their keys: Luke had the iron key, Abigail the crystal, Jemima the silver and Jamie the gold.

'I wrote down all the codes and sequences after our last visit,' said Luke. He pulled a small notebook out of his pocket.

'Clever as always,' said Jamie. 'Come on, let's do it.'

They silently entered the lair. Trigger stood on guard at the entrance. Dougal would stop halfway down the maze. Timber would go all the way to the end with the children. Oberon flew in too.

Gildevard was watching from a distance, out of the range of the garden birds or even Oberon's sharp eyes and ears. He was tucked tightly into the tallest, thickest fir tree he could find, waiting to see what would happen.

The children used torches and wand tips to light their way through the dark passages. The iron key opened the granite slab at the back of the lair once again. They went through the gap and crept carefully along the low, narrow passage till they reached the next stop. The crystal key opened the matching crystal lock on the small wooden door, but the silver key wouldn't open the third lock once they reached it.

'What's the matter with my key?' asked Jemima, trying it again.

Timber sniffed around the lock. No one else had been there, no one with any scent anyway.

Luke checked his notebook. 'I didn't get it wrong,' he insisted. 'I definitely pressed the symbols in the right order. But something is different. Oh! Oooh!' He looked closely at the ornate little door.

'What is it?' asked Jamie.

'Wait! I need to check something.' Luke peered at the symbols in the dim light, checking his notebook several times.

Timber suddenly realised what the problem was. He barked at Oberon, then lunged forward to block

Jemima from trying her key a third time.

'Nobody move!' cried Abigail, spotting another problem.

Everyone got a fright. They each jumped, bumping into each other and the walls of the narrow passage. Timber was turning in circles in front of the door, and Oberon's loud hooting was amplified in the tight space. It was very uncomfortable.

'Crikey!' cried Jamie. 'Timber, settle down.'

'Oberon, shh,' said Luke.

'Don't try the key again till we're sure about the symbols,' said Abigail. 'If we turn it a third time and the codes are wrong, we could set off a booby trap.'

'The symbols have changed, haven't they?' said Jemima.

'Yes, they have,' said Luke. He sounded both annoyed and surprised, like he should have expected it.

'Dark magic did this,' said Abigail. 'The Protection charms will test us differently at every stage. We were lucky the first two hadn't changed.'

'So each door could have a different puzzle from now on,' said Jemima.

'Yes,' said Abigail. 'It might be the symbols on the

door, the way the key turns in the lock – anything.'

'Wow, I thought it would be easy because we had been here before,' said Jamie.

'So did I,' said Luke. He leaned closer to make sure he had it right this time. When he was certain of the new sequence, he pressed the new combination and Jemima turned the silver key. The door opened and they moved on to the fourth stage.

At the next door, they were careful to check everything first and found not only a change in sequence but extra puzzles and codes to decipher too. It took Luke a lot longer to figure them out, and everyone was getting hot and nervous as the minutes ticked by. Timber was panting with the heat. Oberon tried fluttering his wings to provide a little relief but it wasn't nearly enough.

Finally they were ready. The last little door slid open and revealed the tiny cave, the stone with the paw print and the second sliding stone that hid the orb.

Timber trotted in first, relieved to see that the orb was untouched. He pressed his paw on the stone on the ground, and the second stone in the wall slid to one side. A third flat stone emerged slowly out of the wall, the orb sitting on top of it. Bright light bounced around inside it, just like it had before.

Oberon tucked in beside Timber. 'So far so good,' he said. 'Is it safe to lift it off that slab?'

'I expect so,' said Timber. 'I hope so. The children will have to carry it.'

Jamie was about to reach for the orb when something terrifying happened.

Outside, Gildevard's patience had worn out. 'Time to find out what's going on in there,' he thought. 'Trigger is very fast. I'll have to fly like a rocket to get past him.'

The eagle plummeted from a height through the trees towards the spot, turned sharply into the lair and straight into the maze. Trigger was so startled he could do nothing to stop the eagle as he whizzed by in a blur. He barked and sped after him down the passageway. Both collie and eagle passed Dougal before he could react, and then he followed too, barking hoarsly with fright and rage.

As the two dogs and the eagle hurtled along the maze, the orb's light went out. The children, Timber and Oberon were surprised, but not only by the disappearing light. They also heard a long, slow creaking sound that quickly rose to a thundering roar. A look of terror spread across their faces.

'What is that?' whispered Jemima.

'I think it's a booby trap,' said Abigail.

The sound grew louder. The children began to think they would be crushed or swallowed up. The owl spun his head full circle to try to find the source of the trouble. Timber growled, then barked and tried to nudge the owl out of the tiny cave, but both Jamie and the orb were blocking a hasty retreat.

The eagle's sharp ears had caught the sound early, and being nimbler than the dogs, he slowed, turned, skimmed the wall and flew back the way he had come. Dougal and Trigger let him go and hurried on to check on the others.

Panic set in. In that tiny cave and narrow maze of passageways, the space was too tight to do anything quickly, even think.

'Leave the orb,' cried Luke. 'We have to get out of here.'

'We can't leave it,' cried Jemima.

'I can get it,' cried Jamie, stretching his arm till it hurt.

'We have to go now!' cried Luke.

It was already too late. The walls were cracking and water was seeping in, slowly at first, dripping, then faster until it was pouring in. The children tried to move back to a wider part of the passage, but their bulky coats slowed them down and their heavy boots were sticking as the ground turned to mud.

Above the noise, they could hear every door they had come through slam shut. They knew of no other way out. The maze was flooding fast and the water was pushing them farther into the cave.

'The Pyramid Tomb,' said Abigail slowly.

The others looked at her in horror.

In a massive gush, the walls split apart, then collapsed. The children, dogs and Oberon were swept violently away on a tidal wave of water.

Chapter Eight

FLOODED

The eagle just managed to escape, but only because he could fly incredibly fast. He burst out of the lair, losing a few tail feathers as the granite stone closed with a heavy clunk behind him. As he caught his breath sitting in a nearby tree, he wondered what was happening deep underground.

The children, dogs and Oberon were swept along tunnels and passageways they hadn't even known existed. Somewhere on the other side of the cave where the orb had been hidden, lay another maze, another and another.

As the water went over their heads, the four children gulped a last breath and tried to hold on to each other. The dogs and Oberon were swept out of reach, then out of sight. In a mangled blur of fur and feathers, they disappeared into the murky swirls of foaming water and mud.

Hurtling along and running out of air, it was difficult to think what to do. Holding hands and arms became more and more difficult as the water moved faster, tossing them about, carrying them forward. As they were flung around yet another bend, Abigail frantically grabbed at Jemima's pocket.

After a few seconds of confusion, Jemima realised that Abigail was trying to reach the gems. She tugged at the pouch till it popped out of her pocket.

Gulping at pockets of air in the narrow space between the water and the top of the maze, and with their arms awkwardly linked, Jemima held the pouch with her free hand and Abigail reached in. The three gems all felt the same, but she had to pick the next one in the sequence or the magic wouldn't work. If ever she needed her gift of knowing, it was now. She concentrated as hard as she could, found a tiny moment of calm, and picked one.

Grabbing the sapphire as tight as she could, she wished for air to breathe. There was a flash and a few bumps, and then the four were floating together in a bubble that bounced wildly along another water-filled passage. The children looked wide-eyed at each other. The magic had worked just in time. But how long would it last? Where would this river take them, and where were the dogs and Oberon?

After a couple of minutes they could feel their air was running out, yet still they continued their journey through the twisting, turbulent, underground waterways. Their throats tightened and their lungs burned as they breathed in the last of the oxygen. Suddenly, and with a terrifying whoosh, the children were thrust into the open air, spluttering, coughing, gasping.

'Whaaaa! Whe-wherrrre are we?' cried Jamie.

Despite their buckling legs and flaying arms, they quickly found they could stand in the water. Once their vision cleared, they knew exactly where they were – in the pond.

'We're b-back, I mean ho-home!' cried Jemima.

'That th-thing tri-tried to kill us!' spluttered Luke.

'Wh-where is it?' gasped Jamie. 'Where's the orb?'

'I don't know,' said Luke, trying to turn left and right. It was hard to move in heavy, wet winter clothes. 'It must have been taken away by the water.'

'But where?'

'Wherever it wants to go,' said Abigail. 'There was dark magic protecting it and more dark magic in that maze.'

'Hey! HEY!' roared Jamie. 'Where are Timber and the others?'

'Weren't they ahead of us?' said Luke.

Jamie looked around frantically and even went underwater again. Nothing. He came up, gasping for air, panicking. Everyone turned when they heard Trigger and Dougal barking hoarsely. They had already clambered out of the pond and were coughing up water on the grass.

'They made it!' cried Jamie. 'But where's Timber? TIMBER!'

'Oberon's missing too,' said Luke.

'We have to find them!' Jamie dived back under the surface, but he was so distressed and his clothes so heavy, he couldn't swim properly at all. Luke pulled him up and they struggled out of the pond. The girls were sitting on the grass, still spluttering. They sat together, utterly exhausted, miserable, shaken. There was no sign of Timber or Oberon.

Once the children had been swept into the pond,

the water began to settle down. Timber had swum back to search for the owl. Oberon had broken one of his wings when he got caught under a slide of mud. As Timber swam towards the owl, he saw the orb floating beside him. He was so surprised he nearly barked, then nearly choked, but had to hold his breath in order to save the owl. Carefully, he took the owl in his jaws and swam away, leaving the orb bobbing eerily behind them.

Timber felt his lungs about to explode as he swam and swam, yearning for the end of the water and somewhere to breathe. At the last moment, close to despair, he burst out of the water.

'TIMBERRR!' roared Jamie, and he jumped back into the pond, stumbling, splashing and yelling. Luke followed him. Jamie hugged Timber tightly, trying to squeeze any water out of his lungs. Luke took the injured owl out of Timber's mouth. They waded to the edge of the pond, placed the owl on the grass and together hauled Timber out. The other animals and birds who had gathered in the breaking dawn looked on, terrified.

'Is Oberon alive?' whispered Jemima.

'I think so,' said Jamie, examining the owl. 'His left

wing is broken but I don't see any other injuries. I'll press his tummy.'

Jamie gave the owl a little squeeze, then a bigger one and Oberon coughed up water. After a few more coughs and gurgles, he was breathing well, dazed, weak, but alive.

'Ernie will heal the wing,' said Abigail. 'Look, he's here.'

The big fat frog hopped over to the owl and worked his healing magic. The goldfish popped their heads out of the water to see what was going on. They had been hiding in the plinth at the bottom of the fountain while the extra water was gushing into their home.

'If it's OK with you, Timber,' said Ernie, 'the goldfish and I would like to go to our winter tank in Jamie's bedroom – today.'

'Good idea,' said Timber, shaking himself vigorously. 'I think Jamie will be thinking the same thing after this.' He coughed up the last of the water and gave a loud howl.

'They're OK,' said Jamie. 'What a relief.'

'We were lucky,' said Jemima.

'Where did all that water go?' asked Luke. 'It was like a tsunami.'

‘Very dark magic,’ whispered Abigail.

‘You did really well to pull the right gem out,’ said Jamie.

Jemima gave her friend a hug. They all knew they had nearly drowned.

Oberon finally stood up without falling down, shook his feathers and tested his repaired wing. The rest of the pets were showing their relief with barking, meowing, tooting and chirping, when they were interrupted by an unexpected voice.

‘What’s all this?’ asked Greg.

‘Dad!’ cried Jamie. ‘Um, we all fell into the pond.’

‘At this hour?’ said Greg.

Thaddeus hurried out from the house. Nura, his house nightingale, was fluttering on his shoulder.

‘Granddad!’ cried Abigail. She ran over to greet him and Jemima ran to her father.

‘The owl nearly drowned, Dad,’ said Jamie. ‘We were just trying to save him, well, Timber saved him really, but . . .’

‘I’m sorry, Jamie, Jemima, I have to mesmerise your father, just a little,’ said Thaddeus, as he waved his wand. It sputtered and fizzed as he cast the memory mist.

Greg immediately smiled, yawned and looked drowsy.

'He saw you coming out of the pond and knew it wasn't some silly dawn swim, not at this time of year,' said Thaddeus. He held Greg's arm and turned him towards the house. 'You can tell me all about it later. Greg should lie down for a while, and your mother is still in a very deep sleep.' Thaddeus looked at Abigail. 'I think it's time you had some lessons with your aunt Tamara as well as me.'

The children followed Thaddeus and Greg inside.

'How much trouble do you think we're in?' whispered Luke.

'Loads,' muttered Jamie. 'With everyone.'

To their surprise, sweet smells of chocolate, cookies and muffins filled the warm kitchen. Esther had a wonderful way of baking treats in no time at all, even when her wand was wonky. She looked relieved to see them.

'I'll take your father up to bed,' said Thaddeus. 'He'll be fine in a couple of hours and he won't remember anything, with a bit of luck. Each of you needs a hot bath, some hot chocolate and at least one of Esther's magic muffins. Don't worry, they'll make sure you don't catch cold, nothing more.'

'Thanks, Professor. Thanks, Mrs Allnutt,' said Jamie. 'I'll just go and look after the dogs first.'

All the explanations had to wait till later in the day, as Thaddeus had to hurry to the Eastern Woods. He had dropped by the house because Nura had been in such a tizzy in her cage. She had sensed something was wrong with her friend, Oberon, and the professor and Esther had decided to pop in to the Grindles early. Esther would stay and keep watch for a couple of hours.

Having been up all night, the children were glad to go to bed for a nap, after devouring the muffins and cleaning themselves up. In all the kerfuffle, however, no one had seen the orb.

After a short rest, Oberon rejoined the animals in the garden. Trigger and Dougal told Timber about the eagle barging into the lair. Timber was furious that Gildevard knew about the orb. To everyone's surprise, the eagle responded quickly to Timber's howl. He arrived to an angry crowd.

'The children could have been killed! Trigger, Dougal and Oberon too!' barked Timber. 'What were you thinking, following us like that? Something went horribly wrong down there and I think it was your fault!'

'That's not fair!' cried the eagle.

'Timber's right,' said Oberon. 'You set off a Protection charm. It recognised an intruder and collapsed the maze. It's the only explanation for what happened.'

'The orb doesn't like you,' said Eldric, through a snarl. 'It knows you're up to no good.'

The eagle glared at the fox. 'You're all wrong,' he cried. 'I only want to know if the orb contains special knowledge. That's all I'm interested in – knowledge. What else would I do with an orb? Anything could set off a Protection charm, you know that, Oberon.'

'Keep your voice down!' barked Timber, remembering that Bodric might be spying, though perhaps it was too early for the lazy buzzard.

'How would I move an orb?' asked the eagle, spreading his wings, and lifting one taloned foot after the other. 'I couldn't carry it off to my cliff-top nest. Don't be ridiculous! I just wanted to look at it.'

'Just like the scroll, then,' said Norville. 'Your desire for knowledge causes a lot of trouble.' The hedgehog rolled into a spiky ball.

'That scroll burnt to a cinder in my talons while I was trying to save it,' said Gildevard. 'I helped you then and I'm trying to help you now.'

'By setting off booby traps?' said Teddy.

'Stay out of this, Gildevard,' said Timber. 'I don't want you messing things up and putting the children in danger.' He snorted a few times and scratched his paws on the ground. 'We have a job to do. You're either with us or against us. Which is it?'

The eagle glared at him, then flew off in a very big huff, without answering the question.

❦

Bodric wasn't looking forward to giving Zora his latest update.

'What do you mean the children *might* have it?' cried Zora.

'I didn't actually see what happened to the orb, Your Redness,' said Bodric. 'It was unusually early for me to be there, but I thought the eagle might be up to something, so I followed him. And I was right. The children went to get the orb, the eagle disturbed the magic, and then there was a big flood. This is proof that Gildevard wants the orb for himself.'

'Nonsense!' said Zora. 'Are you jealous of him, Bodric? It wouldn't be the first time.'

The buzzard squirmed but didn't reply.

Zora eyed him for a moment. 'All right,' she said. 'If the eagle doesn't report to me by tonight, I want you to spy on him *and* the orb. Make sure that I am the first to know of its location. Understood?'

The sorceress dismissed the buzzard and slammed the door after him. Out in the hallway, Bodric sighed. What he thought would be a simple way of winning Zora's favour had become so complicated.

Everything was about to get more complicated; the goblins were increasingly interested in the orb too.

'So, the rumours are true,' said Krag. 'The orb does exist, and it's not far away.'

'We should take it,' said Dregs, 'as compensation for all our trouble.'

Several goblins cheered in agreement. Claw and his close-knit group did not.

'It is said to have magic never seen or heard of before,' said Dregs. 'It could be worth a lot, or we could pretend it is and trade it for an entire gold mine!'

More cheering.

'The gold lattice that surrounds the orb was made by goblins, from very fine gold,' said elder Rerm.

Krag scratched his scruffy black beard while he thought about it. 'Enough jabbering! I'll give you my decision on the orb later. Right now, we have a visitor.'

A cloaked figure bowed to the goblin king.

'Thank you for receiving me, Krag. I am sure Claw filled you in on our earlier meeting.'

'I have questions,' said Krag, getting straight to the point. 'What else do you know about our missing gold?'

'Only that I think I know who took it, and –'

'You already said it was a Grindle!' roared the king. 'What else?'

'But I didn't say who was going to steal it next,' said Audmund.

Silence.

'Sit,' said Krag, eyeing his visitor suspiciously. 'I'm listening.'

Audmund settled into a chair and began to spin a web of lies.

Chapter Nine

DARK REMNANTS

The children joined the animals and birds at the end of the garden. They couldn't understand all the barks, meows and bird chatter, but they hoped to get some idea of what the animals were planning. They also had a question for them.

'Did any of you see the orb?' asked Jamie, looking around at all the keen faces.

Timber growled and woofed, then shook his ears – his new way to say 'no' and show that he was cross too. Oberon looked frustrated, which probably meant 'no' as well. Dougal and Trigger looked at each other, a bit bewildered. Although all four of them had been in the flood with the orb, none of them had seen where it had gone.

‘It must have been washed away,’ said Jemima.

‘But where?’ said Jamie.

Jemima shrugged.

‘I don’t get it,’ said Luke. ‘How could we lose it?’

They looked at Abigail for her ideas, but she just shook her head.

‘It could be buried under a whole pile of mud, and we’ll never find it,’ said Jamie. He knelt down beside Timber and rubbed the dog’s ears. ‘We are in so much trouble. Not you, not the pets, just us four.’

‘We were just doing what we thought was right,’ said Abigail. ‘We need to know who or what set off the Protection charm.’

The dogs and foxes growled.

‘They know who it was,’ said Jamie, a little surprised. He followed the animals gaze upwards. ‘Up there?’

‘A bird?’ said Jemima.

‘The eagle,’ said Luke. ‘He was outside the lair before.’

‘That’s right,’ said Jamie. ‘But where’s the orb?’

They looked at each other blankly. Timber barked to the pets, telling them he had seen it alongside him in the water as he rescued Oberon. All the pets turned towards the pond.

'Look,' said Jemima. 'They must think . . .'

The children also turned and stared at the pond.

The animals and birds chattered with excitement. Timber scratched his paws on the ground, warning of danger. He lifted his head and howled to call the swans. They could look under the water with their long necks. The children and the pets walked over to the pond and looked in.

'It was floating beside me, like it was watching me,' Timber barked to the animals.

'Floating?' said the Brigadier. 'I thought it would be heavy, made of glass.'

'Watching?' said Ramona.

'Magic explains everything when nothing else does,' said Eldric.

'I don't like that orb,' said Oberon, ruffling his forehead feathers. 'There's something odd about it.'

'No wonder Oscar and Othelia got rid of it,' said Dougal. 'I'll bet they found it was more than they could handle.'

'Maybe they wished they hadn't created it at all,' said Norville.

Timber sat down on the grass. He looked as troubled as everyone else.

'What is it, Timber?' asked Teddy, giving him a little nudge with his nose.

'I'm not convinced this orb belongs in Grindlewood, not to the Wandeleis, not to anyone.'

'What do you mean?' asked Sylvie.

'The queen warned us about it,' said Timber. 'She said it's rumoured to have bewitching powers.'

'And dark magic protects it,' said Oberon. 'That doesn't make it evil, but it isn't exactly a good thing either.'

'And the Wandeleis?' said Teddy.

Timber looked at him. 'If it really does have super power, should anyone have it? It's bound to cause trouble, even wars, like it did before.'

'But someone has to take possession of it,' said Oberon, 'if only to keep it out of the wrong hands.'

The animals fell silent. It was the first time Timber seemed to doubt the queen and her clan.

'Listen up,' said Teddy. 'The children have an idea.'

They were talking about how they could trawl the pond with their fishing nets.

'It'll be very cold and messy,' said Jemima.

'And possibly dangerous,' said Luke. 'The pond might be very deep now. All that water must be somewhere, magic or not.'

'We have to look for the orb. We can't tell the queen we lost it,' said Jamie. 'How did this quest get so messed up?'

'Before you blame me, I did *not* get those codes or puzzles wrong,' said Luke.

'I never said you did,' said Jamie.

'You sort of hinted,' said Luke.

An argument broke out between the boys. Timber howled at them to stop, and then another row broke out among the pets.

'Gildevard should be banished from the garden forever,' said Eldric.

'Is that really necessary?' asked the Brigadier.

'Don't tell me you trust that pompous bird?' cried Norville.

'Timber already sent him packing,' said Ramona. 'Surely, he won't come back.'

'We might need his help, you know,' said Sylvie.

'We can manage without him,' said Norville.

'But can we trust him?'

'No!'

'We might have to!'

'No, we don't!'

'He knows things.'

'So what?'

Timber howled very loudly and this time all the arguing stopped. 'We must not fight amongst ourselves,' he barked, then snorted frequently as he stomped around the group. 'This has never happened before, no matter what the danger. What's wrong with everyone?'

'Please, stop!' cried Abigail suddenly. 'This is what happens with dark magic.'

Everyone stared at her, even the pets. They all wanted to understand what she meant.

'What do you mean, *this*?' asked Jamie.

Abigail explained. 'Remnants of dark magic come with every dark magic event. We have had three: Zora, Worfcus, and whatever is protecting the orb. The remnants upset the balance of everything. We're all affected, even the pets.'

'Makes sense,' said Jemima.

The boys nodded, though they were still feeling cross, and not entirely sure it made total sense to them.

‘I think Abigail’s right,’ Oberon tooted to the animals. ‘I’ve heard of magic unsettling the universe, but I thought it was only a myth. Perhaps it’s true.’

‘Unsettling?’ said Timber, snorting crossly. ‘We have an evil sorceress back from banishment, her wicked twin brother back from Warlock Hell, a band of warlocks and traitors plotting and scheming, goblins stirring, a massive flood that nearly killed some of us and a missing orb that’s using dark magic to save itself at any cost. Yes, I think the universe is trembling.’

The animals had never seen Timber so cross, and he continued to pace around the group.

‘You forgot the Wandeleis’ fading magic,’ said Norville sheepishly.

‘It’s a long list,’ said Teddy crossly.

The hedgehog shook his spines.

‘Enough!’ barked Timber. ‘All arguing stops now. Our enemies would be delighted to know we are squabbling, because it will weaken us and strengthen them. We cannot let that happen.’

The animals mumbled their apologies.

‘When the Wandeleis renew their magic, the balance of light and dark should be restored,’ said Oberon. ‘I think I’m right about that too.’

'Good,' said Timber. 'Let's hope it happens soon. Back to your patrols, everyone. I'll stay with the children and see if they find anything in the pond.'

When the children saw that the pets had calmed down, they ran to fetch the fishing nets.

'We'll need waders,' said Luke. 'That water is too cold without them.'

"We might need these too,' said Jamie, grabbing two pairs of goggles.

'Uh oh, we've got company,' said Jemima, looking over her shoulder at the open shed door.

The butterflies fluttered about for a while as the children collected what they needed. Then they followed them back to the pond where they delivered their message.

Othelia's Orb is not just a treasure,
It holds magic and mystery in equal measure.
Tread carefully now, pay heed to its charms,
With one wrong move, you will set off alarms!

'That message is a bit late,' said Jamie. 'Someone already set off the alarm.'

'We were away from the garden for a while,' said

Jemima. 'I'm sure they would have told us earlier if they could.'

'And it's still a warning,' said Luke. 'We should watch out for more booby traps.'

The butterflies flew off down the garden. The boys pulled on the waders. There were only two adult pairs, so the boys put them on as they had bigger feet than the girls, but it was difficult to walk without falling over.

Timber greeted four pairs of swans and Cyril the heron, who had flown in from Lindon Lake with them.

'The children are about to search the pond for the orb,' said Timber. 'Will you swim around and see if you can spot anything beneath the surface? The boys won't be able to stay in the water as long as you can.'

Cyril and the swans slid into the pond and swam around in different directions. Every so often, they plunged their long necks and heads under the water, scanning for the orb. It wasn't long before Serena spotted something. 'Over here!' she cried. 'In among the reeds.'

Timber and Dougal jumped straight in and

ducked under. The children watched as the two dogs swam around, bobbed up for air then went under again. The heron got out of their way and perched on the fountain, but continued to peer into the water below. The rest of the swans circled the dogs.

'Looks like they beat us to it,' said Luke.

'We should take a look anyway,' said Jamie.

The girls knelt down at the side of the pond, wands lit and pointed downwards, hoping to throw more light on what was beneath. The boys dropped carefully into the water, then moved steadily along the side of the pond towards Timber and Dougal.

When they reached the spot, the dogs were very excited. They had found the orb. Jamie and Luke prepared to look under the surface. They pulled down their goggles, pinched their noses and stuck their faces into the chilly water. A tiny sliver of light pierced through the foliage on the pond floor. As they waded closer, pulling back the reeds to get a better look, the orb rolled further away. It happened again and again, till it reached a deeper part of the pond and the boys had to stop.

'We can't go down there,' said Jamie, gasping. 'Wow, that's cold!'

'It won't let us go near it,' said Luke. 'Whoa! It's really freezing.'

'I just said that,' said Jamie.

'No, I mean it's *really* freezing, look!' Little crystals of ice were forming around the edges of the pond.

'You're right,' said Jamie. 'I'd better take the frog and the goldfish out right now.'

'Quick!' cried Jemima. 'Here comes Dad!'

The boys waded to the edge and climbed out awkwardly, tumbling over in the baggy waders.

'Hi, Dad,' said Jamie as casually as possible. 'I, um, we were just trying to take the frog and goldfish out, but we couldn't find them.'

'Didn't you two get soaked already?' asked Greg somewhat absentmindedly.

'Probably,' mumbled Jamie.

'My head's a bit groggy,' muttered Greg. 'I'll get the tank out of the barn and bring it upstairs for you later. I need to grab some coffee. Then I have to visit the mill about that new job before I start tomorrow. Behave while I'm out. I won't be long.'

'Sure, Dad,' said Jamie. 'We're coming in now.'

'Please get Timber and Dougal out of the pond.

They'll both need a good rub down.' Greg walked quickly back to the house. 'Your mother is lying down. She has a dreadful headache,' he called over his shoulder. 'And Esther is on her way over with a new herbal tea. Bye!'

The dogs hopped out and shook their coats. The boys returned the waders and the goggles to the shed before towelling the dogs dry. Jemima and Abigail stayed by the edge of the pond, hoping to catch another glimpse of the orb, but it remained hidden amongst the thickest reeds in the deeper water.

A short while later, the children gathered in the fairy house.

'Well, we know where the orb is,' said Jamie. 'That was a relief for about five minutes. Now we have another problem, the same one we've had since the start: we can't move it until we decide where to put it.'

'We can't move it if it won't let us,' said Luke.

'At least it's not lost,' said Abigail. 'And we can keep an eye on it.'

'Hiding places, anyone?' said Jemima.

The discussion went in circles again and quickly became an argument as they each had different ideas about what to do. Suddenly, Abigail burst into tears and ran out of the fairy house. Esther arrived, and after seeing to Gloria she took Abigail home. Jemima was upset because she hadn't been able to comfort her friend. The boys sat in silence on the porch of the fairy house, both of them in a huff.

Timber was worried. All these disagreements would only lead to more mistakes, and it was about to get worse. As he trotted back to the pond, Gildevard landed on the grass.

'I heard there was a flood,' he said. 'Is everyone all right?'

'Who told you that?' asked Oberon.

The eagle ignored the owl. 'Are they looking for something in particular?' Two pairs of swans were circling the pond, and Cyril sat motionless on the fountain, staring into the water.

'I told you not to interfere,' said Timber.

'I'm not,' said the eagle. 'I was asking if everything is all right.'

'No you weren't,' said Oberon. 'You were sticking your beak in again!'

Suddenly, Gildevard flew at the owl and the two of them came to blows. Timber knocked them apart with his paws.

The two birds landed on their backs, surrounded by a scattering of feathers.

'Stop it!' barked Timber. 'Dark magic is having a bad effect on everyone and if we can't stay peaceful, we will have to stay apart. Gildevard, leave the garden now. I'll howl if I want you.'

The eagle glared at him and flew off in silence. It was the second time Timber had dismissed him, and his pride was hurt.

'Oh, I am sorry,' said Oberon. 'I shouldn't have lost my temper. That eagle makes me so cross sometimes.'

'Are you injured?' asked Teddy. The eagle was a lot bigger than the snowy owl.

'I'm all right, Teddy, thank you. Just cross, very cross.'

Oberon marched up and down on the grass, trying to calm himself, plucking at feathers, scowling all the while. The rest of the animals started arguing about the eagle again. Timber had to howl several times for quiet. He issued new instructions to keep everyone busy, and took up his position guarding the pond with Teddy. The swans continued swimming round and round, keeping an eye on the orb.

'I'm glad the swans can still come to help,' said Timber, 'but the ducks are safer on Lindon Lake.'

'They've had a lot of to-ing and fro-ing between the pond and the lake this year,' said Teddy. 'But when the next battle begins, will anywhere be safe?'

'I think it will happen here in the garden,' said Timber. 'But not all of us can fight the Worfagons and their allies. That would be slaughter.'

'You think it'll be that bad?' asked Teddy.

Timber looked at him but didn't answer. 'The smaller birds can do the scouting,' he continued, 'but I don't want them involved in any fighting. I'm not even sure if Ernie or the rabbits should be here.'

'We may need Ernie, and Ramona will insist,' said Teddy.

'I know, I'm still considering everything,' said Timber. After a moment, he asked, 'What do *you* think, Teddy? Was Gildevard really concerned about us, or was he just snooping?'

'Hard to say,' said Teddy. 'If he knows about the flood, he probably knows we have the orb. Do you think he will tell?'

'I should have warned him not to,' said Timber, 'but I thought it better he left quickly.' He gave

Teddy a worried look, and they continued their circle of the pond in silence.

As darkness fell, the wind dropped and a strange calm fell over the garden. Down in the pond, the orb was glowing, sending shafts of coloured light across the pond floor. After a while, the light faded and the water got colder and colder.

Chapter Ten

DANGEROUS GAMES

Audmund thought his meeting with the goblins had gone well. It was late when he returned to the manor but he had one more thing to do before he retired to bed.

Once he was sure the coast was clear, he put on his cape and headed off to the forest outside the manor's wall.

He found the tree and slowly climbed it. About half way up, he stopped and thrust his hand into a deep crack in the trunk. Stretching his long fingers, he reached in for the two copied keys.

But they were gone.

'The wretch!' His first thought was of Vargon. 'But no. It can't have been him.' Next, he considered

Worfeus. 'No, he is fussing over his army. Drat! Who took my keys?'

He shook his fist at the sky, forgetting where he was for a second, and slid all the way down to the ground, tearing his cape and scratching his hands. He skulked back to the manor, furious and concerned.

Worfeus returned the next day, sooner than expected, and he was in high spirits. He had found large numbers of warlock warriors, who he was convinced were overjoyed to see him. It was more likely they were looking for something to do that might relieve their boredom. Delighted with his success, Worfeus put on his finest clothes and kept his appointment with King Krag.

The goblin realm was a strange one, attached to all worlds, magical and non-magical. Only dark magic allowed visitors over the invisible suspended-dimension bridge without a goblin escort. Newly returned from the darkest place of all, Worfeus had no trouble arriving into the goblins' territory without an escort, much to their annoyance.

'Hello, Krag, you must have heard that I'm back from Warlock Hell.'

The goblin king did not react; neither did his horde.

'Yes, well, I've come with a proposal,' Worfeus continued. 'I'm sure you already know that this orb we're keen to find is covered in gold lattice, undoubtedly made by your ancestors as all fine pieces of gold are. I'm willing to guarantee its return to you in exchange for your assistance in putting an end to our mutual enemies, the Wandeleis.'

'Is that so?' said Krag.

'It is,' said Worfeus. 'And you'll also get a chance to hammer a few dwarfs while you're at it. What do you say?' He beamed at his unresponsive audience.

'I smell a rat,' said Krag. 'Why don't you deal with your enemies yourself?'

'My sister and I have a few other matters to settle,' said Worfeus. 'If we work together, we could get this business over quickly, settle a few old scores, share the spoils of victory and then go on our merry, but separate, ways.'

'When is this great battle for supremacy going to happen?' asked Krag.

'Zora is still a little under the weather, but soon, Krag, very soon,' said Worfeus. 'We want to make sure we are all in tip-top shape so that our victory is decisive and swift. If you agree, we can shake on it and

I'll be in touch closer to the time.'

Krag gave a slight nod and a snarl, but didn't offer his hand; goblins didn't like shaking hands. Worfeus took that as agreement and departed. But some of the goblins were angry with their king.

'Why should we get mixed up in their war?' shouted Dregs. 'We should take the orb and the lattice, then leave them to it.'

'I told you, I've heard about this orb, and I've a feeling we should find it before they do,' said Krag. 'The magic inside it isn't ours, but that's what intrigues me. And if it includes crushing a few dwarfs, why not?'

Most of the horde laughed.

'The Wandeleis have a long and nasty history with the Worfagons,' said Claw. 'This could drag on.'

'If we're in on the action from the start, we have a better chance of finding what we want: the gold lattice and our lost gold. After that, those two clans can fight it out by themselves.'

'What about our agreement with Audmund?' asked Dregs.

'Agreement?' roared Krag. 'I don't make agreements. They're all after the same thing: magic and power. We'll use any *agreements* to suit ourselves.'

'Worfeus is back from Warlock Hell,' said elder Rerm. 'He could be a threat.'

'Don't worry,' said Krag. 'Worfeus may think he's powerful and clever, but he was always a buffoon and I don't think he has changed. Despite what our visitors say or think, they're all wrong about one thing: *we'll* be taking the spoils of battle, including that precious orb.'

Back in Mord Manor, Vargon was in his study, gulping down potions. He slammed a goblet down on his desk. 'How dare they?' he cried. 'That orb is rightfully mine. I am Oscar's great-great-great-great, oh whatever, grand-nephew, his only living relative! Yet all of them ignore me and my plan. *My* plan! BAH! And now Audmund has brought the goblins in on it too. Why did he involve that treacherous lot? What a mess this has become. AGHHHH!'

He stormed into the parlour where Worfeus and Audmund were waiting. Zora always arrived last.

'Goblins! What were you thinking of?' Vargon bellowed.

'I thought they could help, My Lord,' said

Audmund. 'I've seen what the Grindlewood Army can do, and we should not forget the prophecy. The goblins will be a distraction, which can only help our cause.'

'A distraction,' said Vargon. 'I wonder if they see it like that. And I know about the prophecy, Audmund, it's about a dog! A DOG!'

'A very particular dog,' said Audmund, 'chosen by the Ancients for this realm. Everyone believes that dog is Timber, even if you don't.'

Vargon huffed and puffed, trying to control his temper before replying. 'Those goblins are a greedy bunch, a devious lot, and they'll want the orb when it comes down to it. Mark my words. We'll all be fighting over it. I admit the warlocks are unreliable, but they should be able to create enough mayhem to keep the Wandeleis occupied. The goblins will just get in the way, *our* way.'

Vargon wobbled slightly, then slumped into his armchair. Zora whirled into the room. Unlike her tutor, she was recovering steadily.

'What seems to be the problem?' she asked,

looking at all the grumpy expressions.

'Audmund has been trading favours with the goblins,' said Vargon, through gritted teeth.

'How embarrassing, Audmund. What were you thinking?' said Zora. 'Well, Bodric has just told me the children have the orb.'

Audmund rolled his eyes. Then a worrying thought struck him: what else had that buzzard been up to? Poking around in the trees, perhaps?

'Never mind Audmund's meddling,' said Worfeus. 'I have a *guarantee* from Krag that his horde will assist us in exchange for taking the gold cover from the orb – we don't want it anyway – and then they'll go away.' He waved his hand dismissively in the air.

'Not you as well!' cried Vargon. 'Why can't you leave the goblins out of this? We have enough to be dealing with.'

'They're bound to get wind of what we're up to while they're lurking around Grindlewood,' said Worfeus. 'Better to have them on our side than against. Though you really should have told me you were talking to them, Audmund.' Worfeus glared at him so hard that Audmund felt his collar tighten.

'So, this is your ace card, is it? said Vargon, looking

from Audmund to Worfeus. 'Goblins? And you believe them?'

'Call them loyal reinforcements,' said Worfeus. 'Loyal to me, anyway.'

It was more irritation than Vargon could bear and he was suddenly overcome by a long bout of coughing. His carefully laid plans were in tatters.

Glad of a reason to change the subject, Worfeus spotted something on the table beside Vargon. 'Is that my old wand?'

Vargon reached for the wand, but Worfeus called it and it whipped through the air to him. It was another disappointment for the old lord; he had hoped that the elder wand had switched allegiance to him in Worfeus' absence, but apparently not.

'So, it is yours,' said Zora. 'Bodric said the squirrel found it.'

'Squirrel?' asked Worfeus.

'Never mind. He ran away,' said Audmund. He didn't want to talk about the squirrel. He had secretly enchanted the shunt stone around Ripley's neck. It allowed him to hear everything Ripley heard, and information might mean the difference between success and failure. Audmund made an excuse to leave and moved quickly towards the door.

'Just a minute,' said Zora.

Audmund stopped, feeling decidedly uneasy.

Zora walked over and stared at him, as beads of sweat ran down his brow. 'The eagle brought me a little present today. Two little presents, in fact. Do you recognise them?' She opened her hand to reveal the copied silver and gold keys.

Audmund's stomach did a flip.

'You *do* recognise them.'

'I thought it prudent to copy the keys in case they were lost or stolen,' said Audmund. He knew he was in a right pickle now.

'Is that so?' said Zora.

Worfeus called the keys with his wand.

'These trinkets won't work,' he said. 'The real keys will have enchantments, unlike these fakes. But of course, the goblins won't tell you that. They just copy them and take your payment. Ha!' He tossed the keys onto the side table. Audmund was seething and struggled to keep his cool.

'If the children do have the orb, you've both wasted your time with the goblins,' said Zora. She leaned close to Audmund and whispered to him, 'I'll be watching you very closely from now on, Audmund, closer than anyone ever did. You'd do well to remember that.'

Audmund muttered another excuse and went to his room. Vargon struggled out of his armchair and went upstairs too. Neither of them slept very well that night.

Chapter Eleven

PUZZLES

Luke was neglecting his archery practice. He was trying so hard to crack a few more pieces of the queen's giant puzzle that he often lost track of time and arrived late. It was causing a lot of friction with Jamie. Abigail was so upset after their last argument that she hadn't visited for days, nor had she been to school. Jamie and Jemima were hardly speaking to each other. They had completely different views on what to do with the orb, not to mention who had upset Abigail the most.

Thaddeus decided it was time to intervene. At the next magical learning lesson, the boys arrived grumpy, the girls silent. Thaddeus smiled as they all sat down, but his gold tooth had lost any persuasion power. He would have to talk them out of their bad humours. 'When someone returns from Warlock Hell,' he said, 'dark remnants accompany them into this world too. The balance of magic is disrupted everywhere, and it affects everyone's mood. The universe will find its balance again once the Renewal charm is done. In the meantime, we must all make a special effort not to let bad humour take over.'

The children shifted uneasily in their seats but didn't reply.

'Now look,' said Thaddeus. 'It's important that you put any bad feelings aside and look after one another like you've always done. Remember the battles you fought, the danger you faced, the risks you took to protect each other. You are friends. You are the *worthy*. So much depends on you.'

'I explained that already, Granddad,' said Abigail. 'But it didn't help.'

'Waiting around is driving us crazy,' said Jamie.

'Then we found the orb and had to keep it a secret while we tried to figure out what we should do,' said Jemima.

'We nearly drowned in that tomb,' said Luke.

'Yes,' said Thaddeus. 'It is certainly your most difficult quest yet.'

'What about those bones, Professor?' said Jamie. 'They're still in the cellar, and with the magic fading, that Concealment charm is bound to wear off.'

'It was only ever a temporary measure to buy some time,' said Thaddeus. 'There has been so much to do. Peabody will be here soon. He will give me a hand, and he says he has something interesting to tell us.'

'I hope it's good news,' said Jamie.

'Try to keep busy with your lessons,' said Thaddeus, 'in normal school as well as all the magical stuff. Luke, I hear you've missed a few fencing classes.'

'Sorry, Professor, I was trying to finish more of the puzzle, but I just kept going in circles.'

'You know it's not a priority for you any more, don't you?'

Luke looked uncomfortable. He always found the puzzle hard to resist.

'All right,' said Thaddeus. 'Show me what you have.'

Luke took some parchment out of his pocket. 'I found something about a flood a while ago, but it didn't make sense until we ended up in the pond.' He opened his notebook. 'There was something about reindeer too, but I didn't get very far with that. The other clue had something to do with Timber. Sorry, Jamie, I didn't tell you because I didn't want to worry you. That's it.'

'Good work,' said Thaddeus. He looked at each of the children. 'Tell me, is there something else?'

'We really don't want to be at normal school, Professor,' said Jemima. 'The whole time we're away from home we keep worrying about what's going on. We need to be keeping an eye on the pets, waiting for the butterflies' messages, ready to go to the Eastern Woods –'

'And watching the orb,' said Jamie. 'We know the Wandeleis want it badly, Professor, but we think it could be dangerous. We can't leave the pets to guard it on their own.'

The others nodded.

'Timber knows what to do,' said Thaddeus. 'But you're right, it could be dangerous. That's why Her Majesty and I kept working on the puzzle, just in case there were any clues about the orb, but not so far.' He took Luke's notebook and the parchment. 'I'll show these to the queen, but make sure you don't miss any more archery classes, OK?'

'OK, Professor,' said Luke.

'And school?' said Jamie.

'I think you're right about that too,' said Thaddeus. 'Magical school is more important right now, though hiding your absence with muffins and chocolate will get trickier as time passes. Leave that to me. Now, before we start today's lesson, I have a message for Abigail. Her Majesty would like you to help Pearl with –'

'*The Book of Darkness*?' Abigail sounded very excited.

'Why, yes,' said Thaddeus. 'She would have asked you herself, but her own preparations are taking all of her time. Pearl really needs your help.'

'When do I start?' asked Abigail.

'This afternoon, if that's all right? I will accompany you.'

Abigail nodded, her heart thumping with excitement, but she was also aware of what it meant for the Wandeleis and the success of the quest.

'Very well,' said Thaddeus. 'Now, Volume 53 everyone, page 799.'

When the children got home, all the animals and birds were busy in the garden, switching patrols, checking the well, watching the orb. Then the butterflies flew in with a new message, a long one.

The magic weakens, the armies gather,
The cracks in the universe show!
Unravel the clues, wield the old willow,
And use all the skills that you know!

The puzzle has clues, and hides many secrets
But all must be ready in time.
The orb is a mystery, shrouded in myth,
Its colours forever sublime!

'The puzzle and the willow,' said Luke. 'Isn't the willow a tree?'

'It could mean the willow wand,' said Abigail. 'Only a queen may use it. It might be an important clue.'

'The goblins keep popping up,' said Jemima. 'Why can't we find them in our books?'

'Their magic keeps them out,' said Abigail.

The others waited for her to explain more.

'It was mentioned in *The Book of Enchantments,*' said Abigail. 'I restored another chapter when I wasn't at school.'

'Will *The Book of Darkness* be difficult to restore?' asked Luke.

'She'll be fine,' said Jamie, glaring at Luke. 'The queen wouldn't have asked Abigail if she couldn't do it.'

'I know,' said Luke. 'But it's the darkest part of the WABOM.'

'Pearl already told me how hard it is,' said Abigail. 'But I'll do my best, I promise.'

'We know you will,' said Jemima.

Chapter Twelve

SPIES

The next morning, while they were having a late breakfast together, Jamie, Jemima and Luke spotted the butterflies in the garden again. Abigail wasn't with them as she was about to begin her work on *The Book of Darkness.* Anxious to hear their message, they ran outside. Timber heard it first.

Sneaky spies watch and hear everything you do,
Tread carefully with all your plans, the how, the what, the who.
The day comes soon when all the magic must be made anew,
And then the orb will only grace the bravest and the true.

After hearing the message, there was a sudden frightful screech overhead, and Gildevard swept down and landed on the ground. 'You should be more careful,' he said to Timber. 'Bodric wears a Worfagon shunt stone. It hides his scent and quietens his paws. He can follow you anywhere without you knowing.'

'We know he's been spying,' said Timber. 'We're being careful.'

'Perhaps not careful enough,' said Gildevard.

'Are you spying too?' asked Eldric.

The eagle glared at him, then turned to Timber. 'The Worfagons are raising a large army and a horde of goblins may be joining them too.'

'Whose side will you be on?' asked Timber.

'If no one trusts me, I will stay on my own.'

Timber was annoyed and started to growl. Trigger and Dougal growled too. Gildevard screeched a warning to them to back off.

'Anything else?' asked Timber through a snarl.

'Zora is growing in strength and is determined to defeat Queen Wanda at any cost,' said the eagle. 'Worfeus is expecting victory to be easy but he's determined to get the orb, then he'll probably try to get rid of his sister. Vargon and Audmund plan to take the orb too, but none of them will want to share it. It's hard to know how this will end, but if you ask me, it won't be good.' With that, the eagle flew off.

The animals went on their patrols with renewed warnings from Timber to stay alert.

The children went into the fairy house. Jamie's frustration finally got the better of him. 'I think we should take another look at the cellar.'

'You know we're not meant to,' said Luke. 'But I would like to do something.'

'We need to know what's down there,' said Jamie. 'Is Abigail coming over soon?'

'I doubt it,' said Jemima. 'She'll be working on *The Book of Darkness* for as long as it takes.'

'Right, well I'm going to take a look,' said Jamie. 'You can stay here or come with me,' and he marched off to the house.

'He's still grumpy,' said Luke.

'There's no point arguing with him when he's in his stubborn mood,' said Jemima. 'But we can't let him go down there alone. Come on.'

They ran after Jamie. Timber followed and he called Teddy too.

It was good timing. Greg had started his job at the mill. Gloria was pressing herbs in the back of one of the barns. Grabbing the torches, the children hurried down to the cellar.

As they moved about the dusty room, they heard the odd sizzle and crack as the Concealment charm Professor Allnutt had placed there finally fizzled out. It left a few small scorch marks on the children's clothes along with a few popped buttons. Timber and Teddy went straight to the bones, sniffing to make sure they hadn't been disturbed, then they left them alone. Next, they moved over to the stacks of boxes and crates, checking every pile of rubble and every corner, sniffing for a similar scent.

'We've missed something,' said Jamie, looking behind some empty boxes. 'The goblins died in here. Whatever they were fighting over should still be here, even traces of it, somewhere.'

'Unless a third goblin took it,' said Luke.

Timber and Teddy suddenly bolted out of the cellar. The children knew it must mean trouble and they raced after them, up the staircase and back out to the garden.

Dougal, Trigger, Cindy, Oberon and the foxes

circled an unwanted visitor – Audmund. Realising time was short and not wanting to be outmanoeuvred, he had decided to search for the orb himself and hopefully make a quick getaway. Suspecting the garden might hold some clues, or even the orb itself, he shunted in. Once again, he found himself pinned down at the well.

'You again!' cried Jemima, rushing forward with her wand, forgetting that it probably wouldn't work. She halted, watching as Audmund tried to untangle himself from the barbed wire. Luke stood beside her with the pets, while Jamie ran on to the fairy house to grab his sword.

The dogs were jumping and barking, making a terrible racket. Audmund struggled awkwardly to remove the barbs from his cloak and arms. Before he could free himself, Jamie returned and lunged with his sword, slicing Audmund's wand in half. Audmund let out a roar, pressed a thumb to his snake-seal ring, roaring louder still as his cloak, hands and arms were cut and torn by the barbed wire. He vanished with a pained expression on his face.

'That's right, run away!' shouted Jamie.

'Coward!' cried Jemima.

There was a sizzle and pop and Audmund's broken wand flamed briefly, then turned to ash.

'We should carry our weapons all the time from now on,' said Luke.

'You're right,' said Jamie. 'Just as well we got out of school.'

'The battle will come soon, won't it?' said Jemima. 'It could be days, even hours away.'

Timber was furious. Audmund had caught them off guard despite all their patrols and his warnings to stay alert.

'He tried it again!' he barked till he was almost hoarse. 'He dared to enter this garden the same way as before. He's after the orb for himself.'

'Everyone must know it's here,' said Teddy. 'They'll all be coming for it.'

Audmund retreated to his study in disgust. 'I can blame Grizzle for all these cuts and scratches,' he thought, 'but I'll have to find another wand. DRAT! How will I explain *that* to Vargon, to anyone?' He washed his cut hands in the sink then prowled up and down his study, thinking. 'All the trouble I went to to get those keys copied, grovelling to those stinking goblins. Now they're useless. DRAT! DRAT! DRAT!' He threw a few books at the wall in temper. 'Time is running out. Zora will be ready soon, and the goblins will arrive. Why do I feel this is not going to turn out well?'

There was a knock at the door. It was Vargon again.

'Bad timing?' he said, pushing past. 'We need to talk.' They sat down opposite each other, both looking the worse for wear. 'Playing with the dwarf-troll again?'

Audmund gave a weak smile. 'As you know, we can't heal every scratch with magic. What is it now?'

'This whole business is getting out of hand,' said Vargon.

'My thoughts exactly.'

'Involving the goblins was rash,' said Vargon. 'If it comes to choosing who to support, they will favour Worfeus over you.'

'No matter what you say, the Worfagon warriors are unreliable,' said Audmund. 'We need the goblins to help take care of the Wandeleis, the Grindlewood Army *and* those horrid dwarfs. You and I can take care of the orb.'

'You don't fool me,' said Vargon. 'You wanted those

keys so you could get to the orb first. Well, that plan backfired.' Before Audmund could defend himself, Vargon continued, 'And did it ever occur to you that despite their horrid history, Worfeus and Zora might start scheming together against *us*?'

'How could Zora forgive Worfeus after he banished her?' asked Audmund.

'Zora will do anything to get what she wants,' said Vargon. 'Once she defeats the Wandelei Queen and takes possession of the orb, who knows what she'll do with its power. Things have gone too far, Audmund. I can't control her anymore. And Worfeus thinks he will be king of Grindlewood. Ha! This is a mess!' Vargon shook his fists in the air. 'You thought bringing Worfeus back would keep Zora in check,' Vargon continued, wagging a ringed finger at Audmund. 'Can't you see that he is using you? He'll dispose of you as soon as he gets the orb.'

'He was stopped before,' said Audmund, though he knew Worfeus would be smarter this time.

'Indeed he was,' said Vargon. 'But there are two of them now, and they are both very determined.'

'All right,' said Audmund. 'What do you suggest?'

'A change of plan,' said Vargon. 'Very soon, those

two will realise they don't need us any more, and we had better be ready.'

Chapter Thirteen

WAITING

When the children and Timber arrived in the Eastern Woods, the professors were sitting with the queen, talking in hushed tones.

'So, the butterflies have confirmed what I suspected,' said the queen, after the children repeated the last two messages, 'but it doesn't help us find the spy in our midst.'

'Ripley!' cried Pendrick, suddenly.

'The squirrel?' said Jamie.

'Isn't he still locked up?' said Sparks.

'Yes. No. Not him, his shunt stone,' said Pendrick. The professor hurried off but returned quickly with a grumpy-looking dwarf who was carrying a cage with Ripley inside. The squirrel looked terrified.

'I didn't know my shunt stone was spying on you,' he cried. 'You took it off me as soon as I got here. I had nothing to do with this, nothing. Audmund made the shunt stones. He gave one to me, one to Bodric and the golden eagle. That's all I know, I swear.'

'Enough,' said the queen impatiently. 'Take him away.'

The dwarf gave the cage a good shake till the squirrel stopped moaning, and then carried him off.

'Good grief!' cried Pendrick. 'Audmund could have heard all our conversations.' He turned to Flint. 'Your wand, please, Professor.'

'Of course,' said Flint. 'But I think it will explode just like yours did earlier.'

'Allow me,' said Wanda. 'The willow will not lose its power like other wands.' She fired a spell at the shunt stone. It broke into several pieces, each one slowly turning black until they looked like tiny pieces of coal.

The queen fell back into her chair. Every time she used the willow it drained her.

'You really should rest, Your Majesty,' said Thaddeus.

'No, I must work, practise and prepare,' said Wanda, trying to get up. She slumped back into her chair again.

'What else did you come to tell me?' She looked at the children, then Timber. They had been very quiet all this time.

'Your Majesty, we think Timber wants to tell you something,' said Jamie.

Timber trotted forward and sat in front of the queen.

'I would like to ask the animals of the Eastern Woods to join us in defending Grindlewood,' barked Timber, in witch language. 'Gildevard told us the goblins will be joining the Worfagons, Worfeus has been rounding up more warriors, and we suspect that Vargon will use his metal hawks, poisonous bats and spiders too. We need more help.'

'You have my permission to ask the stag,' said the queen. The children thanked her and followed Timber into the woods to look for Sebastian right away.

'What a good idea, Timber! Good boy!' Jamie called after his dog, as he trotted ahead of them.

'We could do with their help,' said Luke. 'And more.'

'I doubt if the reindeer leave here much,' said Jemima, looking around. 'I hope the stag won't mind.'

As they walked along the meandering path through

the trees, they marvelled at the beauty of the woods, set as it was in a magical dimension. It was always warm there, and now and then there was a soft breeze. A multitude of scented flowers bloomed all year long, and the incredibly tall trees branched upwards like they were reaching for the sky. When they came to a clearing, the giant stag stood watching them from the far side of a stream.

'Welcome, Timber, Guardian of Grindlewood,' he boomed. 'Swim across and we will talk.'

Before the children knew what was happening, Timber plunged into the river and swam confidently across to the other side. He climbed out and shook himself.

'Sebastian, we need your help,' he said, looking up at the giant deer. 'A great battle is coming and we need reinforcements to protect Grindlewood. Will you allow the herd to leave the woods and join us?'

'We may only leave under special circumstances,' said the stag. 'And our departure from these woods comes at a price. It is the Ancients' law.'

'What is the price?' asked Timber.

'You must promise, Timber, that if any harm should

come to me, you will replace me as Guardian of the Eastern Woods,' said the stag. 'It would mean never returning to Grindlewood. You should think on it carefully before you agree.'

The stag turned away and walked over to the reindeer who were standing nearby. Timber sat down on the grass to ponder the stag's condition. The sun felt warm and soothing on his fur. He thought about how they might cope without the stag's help. He knew the Grindlewood Army was brave, but they were no match for the power and might they would be facing this time. On the other hand, if the reindeer did come to help them and something happened to the stag, Timber would have to keep his promise. Guarding the Eastern Woods didn't trouble Timber, but leaving the Grindles, all his friends and the garden did.

Jamie, Jemima and Luke sat at the edge of the river, watching, but they didn't try to cross.

'What's Timber doing?' asked Luke.

'I'm not sure,' said Jamie, 'but he looks sad. I don't like it.'

Timber looked across the river. He knew he couldn't take a chance with the children's safety. He stood up and trotted over to the stag. 'I agree to your terms,' he said.

'Then we will help you,' said Sebastian. The other reindeer gathered round. None were quite as big as Sebastian, but they were tall and strong and had the same huge antlers. 'Except for a few who must remain here on watch, the herd will be there when you need us.'

Timber howled his friendship howl and swam back to join the children.

Shortly after they returned home, Abigail arrived in the fairy house.

'Is it finished?' asked Luke, as soon as she came in.

'It's *nearly* finished,' said Abigail, blushing. 'I have a few hours off while the inks are setting. It has to be perfectly dry before I can move on to the next bit.'

'How much longer?' asked Jamie.

'I'm hoping to finish before December twenty-first, the winter solstice, the next magical date in the Wandeleis' calendar. If the WABOM is complete, we could hold the Renewal ceremony that day.'

'So close to Christmas,' said Jemima.

'It's been hard to think about Christmas this year,' said Jamie.

'We nearly forgot about our birthdays in October too,' said Jemima, looking at Abigail. 'Mum and Dad thought I was ill or something.'

'If I finish *The Book of Darkness,* it'll be the best Christmas present ever,' said Abigail.

'You'll finish the book,' said Jamie, thinking it through, 'and then the queen will do the renewal. Then what?'

'Then we wait for the Worfagons to, to . . .'

'Attack?' said the boys.

'Where?' asked Jemima.

'The queen wants to move back to Hollow Hill as soon as possible,' said Abigail. 'Bringing a battle to the Eastern Woods would be a terrible disgrace, but I don't think it will be in Hollow Hill either.'

'Where then?'

'Uh oh,' said Luke, figuring it out.

'It might be here,' said Abigail, 'in the garden, but I'm not sure. It's just a guess. I, I don't know for sure, but . . .'

'But the orb is here,' said Jamie.

'And because it's Grindlewood garden,' said Abigail. 'The centre of magic in this world.'

'The what?' said Luke.

'It's in *The Book of Enchantments*,' said Abigail. 'In another part I restored. Look.' She pulled the little book out of her rucksack and opened the page. There were several maps and constellation charts showing Grindlewood garden at the centre.

'That must have been really difficult work,' said Jemima.

'It was,' said Abigail, 'but great practice for what I'm doing now.'

'It would take ages to understand all that,' said Luke, tracing his fingers along some of the lines and charts.

'You can see that this garden is at the heart of it,' said Abigail.

'That's why everything happens here,' said Jamie.

'I wonder if George Grindle figured that out,' said Jemima. 'Maybe he discovered some of Grindlewood's secrets too.'

'We should take a closer look at his notes,' said Jamie, 'and those papers that Dad has been holding on to.'

Jemima went to the bookcase and pulled down some books, including George's diaries and ledgers, and the four of them began searching for more clues.

They didn't really expect to find much, but at least it was something to do.

After telling all the pets about the spies, Ripley's shunt stone, the reindeer and Abigail's progress, Timber privately told Teddy what he had agreed with Sebastian Stag. 'If I have to leave for the Eastern Woods, you would be in charge here, Teddy.'

'But, Timber, Jamie couldn't bear it if you left, none of us could. Where you go, I go, like always.'

'Not this time, my friend,' said Timber. 'I must keep my word. It is the Ancients' law, one that the stag and the herd must obey. If Sebastian is unharmed, I'll be staying right here.'

'Right,' muttered Teddy, but he didn't feel all right.

'Keep this a secret for now,' said Timber, giving Teddy a lick. 'Everyone has enough to think about, but I thought you should know. Everyone seems pleased that the reindeer will be helping us.'

'Sure, great,' muttered Teddy. He looked sadly at his best friend as they trotted off on patrol, hoping the next few days wouldn't be their last together.

The professors returned a little later to see the queen. Now that Abigail was nearly finished her work, they wanted to announce a date for the Renewal ceremony and begin preparations. Wanda looked a little more refreshed after her nap and some fairy brews. It didn't take long to agree on a date, the closest one possible in the magical calendar.

'Yes, December twenty-first,' said Wanda. 'The winter solstice.'

'We'll be lucky if the Worfagons don't attack before then,' said Pendrick. 'They must be almost ready, and if Zora isn't, then maybe Worfeus will come alone – with Audmund, that wretch!'

'We cannot take on the Worfagons without all our magic,' said Wanda. 'And the renewal date depends entirely on how quickly Abigail can finish *The Book of Darkness*. If we miss the winter solstice, we will have to wait till the first of spring.'

'Oh, Merlin's beard!' gasped Sparks.

Flint gulped.

'I believe Abigail can do it,' said Thaddeus.

'So do I,' said the queen. 'But we must make defence arrangements too, even if our magic is restored. Inform the clan, gentlemen, and begin the preparations. We are about to go into a battle foretold by the Ancients. It is unavoidable.'

Chapter Fourteen

THE CRIMINAL COURT

King Krag was facing a revolt. The horde had received word of a major gold find, the first in a long time, and many goblins wanted to leave.

'Which of the Worfagons is telling the truth?' shouted Claw.

'None of them,' roared Krag. 'Our gold is somewhere in amongst their lies and stories, so there is only one way to find out. We are joining the fight in Grindlewood and we will get our lost gold back too!'

'It sounds rather like a *personal* quest to me,' said elder Rerm. 'I understand how you might wish to find gold that was lost during your father's reign. It is a noble idea, but is it wise?'

'How dare you challenge me?' cried the king. 'We

will take back what is rightfully ours and close this chapter of history. Then we will head for the gold mine. Is that clear?'

'We are wasting our time here,' Claw whispered to those beside him.

The grumbling grew louder among the crowd.

Krag had to come up with something else to satisfy the protestors. 'Goblins,' he roared, and the horde hushed. 'I can see you want some sport. Before we enter their battle, why don't we put them all in a goblin CRIMINAL COURT?'

The chamber erupted in cheers and whistles. A criminal court was a treat for the goblins, and it didn't happen often. It was a smart move by Krag. The goblins should get some answers and, with a bit of luck, someone would be tortured or even hanged. That would surely please the complainers.

Krag led his senior goblins to a corner of the chamber. 'We'll take the Worfagons first,' he said. 'Then, we'll go to Hollow Hill and catch the queen and her professors. I've heard they're planning to return there now the dwarfs have tidied it up. Ha! Hollow Hill, that's what they called those tunnels we designed for them, in return for a large cut of the gold we dug up.'

'The very best gold,' said elder Rerm. 'I remember it.'

The ten senior goblins raised their wands till the tips were touching. Krag uttered a few words and they were instantly transported to Mord Manor.

They arrived in the parlour. Everyone they wanted to arrest was present: Zora, Worfeus, Vargon and Audmund. Bodric was already hiding behind an armchair, feeling out of favour, which he was. Gildevard was sitting outside on the windowsill and flew off immediately. He knew better than to get involved in goblin matters.

The Worfagons were taken completely by surprise. Worfeus gave a watery smile and was about to speak when the goblins cast a Binding spell, wrapping the four prisoners in web-like nets, and disabling their magic before they could react. With a few more spells, Zora, Worfeus, Vargon and Audmund were tethered together, lifted off their feet and transported to the criminal court.

'Let them thaw out by themselves,' said Krag when they arrived back to cheers. 'The pain will do them good.'

His horde laughed louder.

'Put their wands in that bucket of swamp sludge so they can't call them. Now, let's get the other lot.'

Krag and company arrived in Hollow Hill in the queen's outer chamber. Queen Wanda and three of her professors were waiting there for Thaddeus to inspect the renovations.

'Good grief!' cried Pendrick, reaching for his wand, which he no longer had. His new one wasn't ready yet, but then neither was their magic. They were in a hopeless position.

'What is this intrusion, Krag?' demanded the queen. 'You cannot enter other domains without invitation.'

'I don't care!' Krag roared back at her. 'I want to know what happened to my ancestors' gold and why everyone is after that orb. You lot are coming with us.'

With a whip of their wands, the goblins took the Wandeleis to their court.

'What is this dump?' asked Zora, as she slowly defrosted. 'And what is that awful smell?'

'Look around,' said Vargon. 'Goblins.'

'I haven't seen this particular chamber before,' said

Worfeus. He sounded mildly amused until he realised he was being held prisoner. 'What? What's this? Why am I tied?' He tried chanting a few spells but they were useless. 'Why can't I undo these binds?'

'Because your magic is not as superior as you think,' roared Krag. 'And I have your wand.'

Worfeus scowled, then he saw the other prisoners, the Wandeleis, all of them still frozen.

'They'll melt soon enough,' said Krag, 'just like you did.'

'This is outrageous!' cried Zora, wriggling hopelessly. 'I am the Red Queen. This is all part of my kingdom. How dare you bind me!'

'QUIET!' roared Krag. 'You have not been crowned queen of anywhere, sorceress Zora. You, your allies and your enemies will answer to my criminal court!'

'Absolutely not!' cried Zora.

'Absolutely YES!' cried Krag.

'This is not good,' muttered Audmund, through gritted teeth. He glanced at Vargon who returned his worried look.

'Goblins are meant to stay in their own territories,' shrieked Zora. 'It's the law.'

'Says who?' asked Krag. 'The Ancients? Guess

what? They're not here any more!' The horde roared with laughter. 'You are in *our* tunnels now, *our* chamber and MY COURT! I'm tired of everyone asking for favours, wanting us to do their dirty work, and then taking what belongs to us!' Krag's face was purple with rage. 'This court will commence NOW!'

The goblins cheered loudly.

'Vargon, what is this place? Where are we?' Zora asked, under her breath.

'I believe we are in a chamber in one of the goblins' tunnel systems,' said Vargon quietly. 'They have dozens of them, that's why we don't see them too often. They like skulking around in the dark, counting their gold, whenever they're not mining it.'

'QUIET!' roared Krag.

'Your Majesty,' said Audmund, 'we had an arrangement.'

'Well, I'm changing it!' roared Krag.

'And *our* arrangement?' said Worfeus, with a smarmy smile.

'Don't push your luck, hell-boy.'

'Sounds like you were both outwitted again,' said Vargon.

'Fools, fools!' cried Zora. 'This is all your fault!'

Wanda and the professors began to stir.

'Oh no! I think I'm in hell,' moaned Sparks.

'Almost,' muttered Pendrick.

'Ahhhchoooo!' Flint sneezed loudly.

Wanda looked fiercely at Krag. 'You must want something very badly to kidnap a real queen.'

'Queens!' snapped Zora.

'Ahem!' said Worfeus. 'I am a king.'

'So the Worfagons have annoyed you. That's no surprise,' said Wanda, ignoring the twins. 'What is it you want?'

'You look dreadful, Wanda,' said Zora. 'I actually look younger than you now.'

'This is not a contest,' roared Krag. 'It is a goblin court, and I am the judge. You will answer all questions to my satisfaction or I will punish you, be you king, queen or otherwise!' He snarled at each of them.

Though short like all goblins, Krag had a ferocious face and an even more ferocious glare. The horde moved closer, forming a tight semi-circle around the prisoners. Krag went to his throne, a crudely-cut wooden chair set upon a slab of rock.

'Interrogator, begin,' ordered Krag.

A weasley-looking goblin stepped forward and

began the questioning in a surprisingly high-pitched squeaky voice. 'First question: what do you know about the fate of the lost crate of gold bars from 1901?'

'Come now,' said Worfeus. 'That's more than a hundred years ago. Why would we care about . . .'

'Answer the question!' roared Krag.

'It has been suggested that this gold is in the cellar of Grindlewood House,' said the interrogator. 'Is this correct?'

No one said anything for a moment.

'Torturers, make ready!' roared Krag.

The interrogator approached Audmund. 'You said one of your spies gave you this information. I ask again, is it true?'

'Well, I think, I mean, it could perhaps, well . . .'

'Is it or isn't it?' roared Krag.

Four goblins were standing close by, holding a long box. It was open and everyone could see its contents: three torturing pincers, eight different sharp hooks, around a dozen claws and several knives of different sizes.

Audmund felt decidedly uncomfortable. 'I can't be absolutely sure,' he muttered, 'but I heard from a source who heard from the animals who heard from the children that the cellar was walled up, so something must have been hidden there. What else but gold?'

Krag glared at him. 'Not so sure about your story now, eh?'

Audmund knew he would have to do better to avoid torture. 'I heard that bones were found. They might be interesting.'

Krag scratched his beard as he thought about it.

'I figured out that shunt stone, Audmund,' said Pendrick. 'Just wait till I get my hands on you, you traitor, you wretch!' He struggled with the web-net but to no avail.

The queen and professors couldn't help thinking again of all the things they had talked about – their plans, their fears, their weaknesses – matters that Audmund might now be aware of. They wondered how much he would give away.

'Move on,' said Krag.

'Next question,' said the interrogator. 'Where is Othelia's Orb?'

'That orb is mine. You can't have it!' said Zora.

Worfeus rolled his eyes.

'Othelia's husband, Oscar, was a Worfagon warlock,' said Vargon. 'It belongs to our clan.'

'Othelia was a Wandelei witch,' said Wanda. 'It is ours.'

'Who cares who made it,' said Worfeus, his anger rising. 'We all know it has to be in that garden.'

'Remind me,' said Zora. 'How do we know?'

'Because everything around here has to do with that garden,' cried Worfeus, impatiently. 'Why don't we just tear the place apart?'

'I'll decide who gets that orb,' said Krag, '*after* we take the gold lattice that surrounds it. It was made by a goblin, and as king, that makes it mine.'

'No, never, all of it is mine!' cried Zora.

'Of course you may take the lattice, Krag, once *we* get the *orb*,' said Worfeus, ignoring his sister's protests.

'Excuse me,' said Audmund, 'but how do you know they can be separated?'

After a moment of confusion, the elder Rerm spoke up. 'I assure you, the lattice will come away from the orb.'

'And if we can't separate them we'll take both,' said Krag.

'What about the other gold, the lost gold?' cried

Claw, his anger growing. Other goblins were getting restless too. The gold bars interested them more than a delicate piece of gold lace, which the king would keep for himself.

'We told you we don't know anything about your gold,' said Zora. 'Foolish of you to lose it in the first place!'

The rumblings grew louder as the goblins took offence.

'What have you to say, old tutor?' said Krag.

The interrogator walked up to Vargon. 'Well?'

'I know that goblin gold went missing long ago,' said Vargon. 'It was presumed stolen, but no one was sure by whom, despite all the rumours. A Grindle lived in the big house back then and he was a very rich man, but I don't know if he was stupid enough to steal from you, or if he needed to.' Vargon began to cough.

'You're not going to last long, are you?' the interrogator whispered to him.

Vargon lifted his head and coughed right at him, and the interrogator withdrew with a snarl.

'I knew George Grindle,' said Pendrick. 'He was a good, kind, hard-working man. He would never have stolen anything from anyone.'

The other professors looked at him. They weren't sure what George had or hadn't done. Rumours had circulated for years, then petered out once the goblins went to explore a new mine. The Wandeleis had hoped the whole episode would be forgotten. It had caused bad feeling among all the magical communities.

'And what of the new family?' asked the interrogator. 'What do they know of George's wealth and the secrets of that house?'

'Whatever happened in the past, that young family has nothing to do with it,' said Wanda.

'But your prophecy says they have a lot to do with the present and the future,' said the interrogator. 'And we all know how that is tied to the past.'

'Why is everyone so obsessed with those children and that dog?' said Vargon. 'We want the orb because it was made by one of our ancestors. Oscar was a brilliant warlock, a genius. He found new magic and captured it.'

'What new magic?' asked the interrogator.

'Well, we, eh, we aren't sure yet,' said Vargon.

There were more grumbles among the goblins.

'Othelia made the orb,' insisted Wanda. 'She was a Wandelei witch.'

'Oscar put the magic in the orb,' said Vargon crossly.

'Enough!' cried Krag. He called his interrogator and three other advisors into a huddle. They mumbled together for a few minutes as the prisoners waited. Mutterings amongst the horde grew very loud. The torturers began polishing their instruments, hoping to be called upon by the king to use them.

Finally, Krag stood up and walked over to the prisoners. 'We will take the gold lattice and any other gold that is found in Grindlewood, even if it means we take the entire orb.' He walked along the line of bound prisoners, stopping first in front of Worfeus. 'You are a liar and a buffoon, and you will never be the king your father was. Your magic comes from the darkest reaches of the underworld, it is true. I can smell it. But it makes you no better than us, so stop acting like you are. I have the measure of you, Worfeus, king of nowhere.'

Worfeus grimaced at the insults but kept quiet for a change. Krag walked on. He ignored Zora, much to her annoyance, Vargon and Audmund too. He stopped again in front of Wanda.

'You claim this orb is rightfully yours, and you believe your clan is favoured by the Ancients. But you are no better than your enemies either. You forget that long ago we witnessed how the wars started, and we were there when crimes were committed by both sides. Don't pretend now that you are so perfect or so chosen.'

Wanda was about to reply but changed her mind when she saw Pendrick's warning stare.

'The prisoners can wallow here for a few more days,' said Krag, turning to face the horde. 'In the meantime, we're going to Grindlewood to check out those stories for ourselves. I intend to finish this once and for all.'

Chapter Fifteen

GOBLIN INVASION

The children were in the fairy house, looking out the window and watching the garden patrols change over. Timber and Teddy were guarding the pond again, Dougal and Trigger were sitting beside the well. Cindy and the foxes were patrolling the perimeter of the garden, while the birds were on watch both inside and further afield. The wind had dropped and the temperature had fallen noticeably; that would create another problem.

'If the pond freezes like last year, we won't be able to get at the orb,' said Jamie. 'Then what?'

'Neither will anyone else,' said Jemima. 'I think Abigail's right. The flood brought it here, so maybe it wants to be here.'

'Is that a good thing or a bad thing?' asked Luke.

'Crikey!' said Jamie. 'I wish we knew how long we have to find a new hiding place. We can't leave it there during the battle. Anyone could steal it.'

'We may have no choice,' said Abigail.

'I wish we knew what to do with the orb,' said Luke. 'I mean, who should really have it, the Wandeleis or the Worfagons? They both made it.'

No one answered that question; it wasn't clear who it belonged to. The other burning question was: what sort of power would it unleash?

'You'd think the Worfagons would strike before the renewal,' said Jamie. 'It would make sense, while the Wandeleis are weak.'

'Hopefully they have as many problems as we do,' said Jemima.

'They don't like to fail or look foolish,' said Abigail. 'That's what the fairies say.'

'December twenty-first is almost two weeks away,' said Luke. 'There was such a mad panic to prepare, and now everything is moving so slowly.'

'Uh oh,' said Jamie. 'Here comes more bad news.'

The butterflies fluttered at the window. Jemima opened it and Edith, Evie and Elle flew around a couple of times before landing with their latest message.

King Krag is a menace; he will have his way,
He gathers the royals to answer or pay.
His verdict depends on what he will learn,
Or else he will punish, torture and burn!

'Who's King Krag?' cried Luke.

Jemima and Abigail went straight to the bookshelves to see what they could find.

'They said "the royals",' said Abigail. 'I suppose that means Zora and Worfeus. Oh no! Queen Wanda too?'

Just then, Bushfire and Jugjaw burst through the trapdoor.

'Thank the stars, you're all here and you're all right!' cried Bushfire.

'Those pesky goblins put us in a Bind-lock and took the queen and the professors,' said Jugjaw.

'Goblins again,' muttered Luke.

'Where did they take them?' asked Jamie.

'Probably to one of their tunnels,' said Bushfire. 'They have lots of them from back in the old days.'

'King Krag is bad news,' said Jugjaw. 'And our magic is rubbish!' He whacked his wand against his boot.

'We couldn't stop them with these silly fiddlesticks.'

'Goblins don't need to renew their magic like we do,' said Bushfire. 'It's so unfair.'

'Where's my granddad?' asked Abigail.

'Sorry, missy, we're not sure,' said Bushfire. 'But he wasn't there when the others were taken, so he's probably fine.'

'Goblins aren't stupid enough to kill royalty,' said Jugjaw. 'They might torture them or, um . . .'

'Ahem, they're probably just after gold,' said Bushfire. 'That's what usually brings them out in such a rage, I mean, fuss.'

'So it *is* about gold,' said Luke.

'But how did they get into the Eastern Woods?' asked Jemima. 'I thought that was impossible without permission or a DimLock like ours.'

'They grabbed the queen and the professors when they were in Hollow Hill inspecting our repairs,' said Bushfire. 'The goblins designed all these tunnels, you see, even the ones we use, so they know where they are and how to get in.'

'But we can't get into their domains without an invitation,' added Jugjaw, with a scowl and another whack of his boot.

'Typical,' said Jamie. 'What can we do now?'

Before the dwarfs could answer, a gang of goblins burst through the trapdoor. Quick as a blink, they bound the dwarfs with magical vines, and pointed their wands at the children's throats.

'Twice in one day, Jugjaw! You must be very cross!' said Dregs. He snarled into the dwarf's face.

More goblins piled into the fairy house, scowling and frowning. Then Krag himself emerged.

'So, you're the new Grindles,' he said. 'Not very impressive, are you?' He looked around the tiny cottage. 'Where's the big snow dog everyone is so afraid of?'

Timber was barking loudly outside the door.

'Don't you dare touch him!' cried Jamie, lunging for his sword.

'Let me see that,' said a goblin, whipping it from Jamie's hand with a swish of his wand. 'Not our craftsmanship,' he said, and he tossed it into the corner.

'Look here!' cried Claw. 'Hector's bow.' He picked it up with the arrows, then tossed them aside too. 'You have been privileged for non-magicals. These gold tips were made by us. Where did you get them?'

'The queen gave them to me,' said Luke.

'Enough chatter,' said Krag. 'You've got something that belongs to us.'

'What? No way,' cried Jamie.

'Show us what you found,' said Krag.

The fairy house was now packed to bursting and every goblin was pointing a wand at the children.

'Or would you prefer if we torture the animals first?' Krag glared at them menacingly, his smelly breath puffing through his wide, hairy nostrils.

'NO! Don't touch them!' cried Jamie. 'We found bones in the cellar, bones and rubbish, that's all. You can look if you want.'

'I intend to,' said Krag.

Timber was going ballistic outside, and now Dougal, Trigger and the Brigadier were barking too.

'Goblins, to the cellar!' roared Krag. 'You, kid, keep those dogs under control or they'll feel my wrath!'

When they opened the door, Jamie immediately ordered Timber to hush and stay down. He reluctantly obeyed and the other dogs followed suit. There was little they could do without endangering the children.

Krag continued to roar orders at the horde. He left one group to search the fairy house. He sent another around the garden, and the rest were split up between the sheds, the barns and the house. All too quickly, there was a shout and their march towards the house halted. The children were turned at wand-point and ordered over to the pond instead.

'Why is the orb shining just when we need it to stay hidden?' barked Dougal.

'How unfortunate!' whined the Brigadier.

'Maybe it's protecting itself,' said Teddy. 'Let's hope so.'

'Timber,' whispered Oberon, tucking in between the dog's front paws. 'I think the pond is icing up.'

'It doesn't usually freeze till January,' said Timber. He looked up and down at the water, trying to spot what the owl had noticed from above. Oberon was right. There was a thin skin of ice around the edges of the pond and a few patches were forming elsewhere too. Something was cooling the water much more rapidly than normal.

'There's nothing we want in that tiny cottage,' said Dregs, returning to Krag's side.

The king had noticed the glow under the water. 'Maybe not,' he said, 'but I think there's something down there.' He raised his wand and tried spell after spell, but the orb didn't come to the surface. 'You two, check it out!' Krag pushed two goblins into the pond. They gasped as they hit the icy water and hurriedly swam around to check what was there.

'There's a r-round sh-sh-shhhh-shiny b-b-ball with a g-g-gold la-la-la-lace th-thin-th-thingy,' said one, shivering uncontrollably.

'That's the orb, you numbskull! Bring it up.'

The children tried not to let their groans be heard, nor show the dismay they felt. They watched anxiously as the goblins tried but failed to remove the orb from the pond.

'Out of my way!' bellowed Krag, and he blasted more spells into the water.

Nothing happened for a moment, then a wave came hurtling out of the pond and drenched half the goblins who were watching.

'Aaaaagh!' roared Krag. 'So the orb doesn't want to move! Get back down there, take the gold lattice off it and bring it to me.'

Again, the goblins failed. 'It will not come off,' said one. 'And I can't feel my feet any more!'

'The water is icy but the orb burned me!' cried the other, holding up a blistered, red hand.

'What kind of magic is this?' muttered Krag. Some of the horde were looking at him suspiciously; goblin magic was rarely outdone.

Suddenly, Jemima burst with frustration. 'The orb doesn't belong to you. Leave it alone and get out of our garden!'

'Nice one, Jem!' said Jamie.

Krag whirled around. 'It certainly doesn't belong to YOU!'

'We don't have any gold, not yours, not anybody's,' said Jemima.

'We were robbed in Grindlewood and it's time for payback,' roared Krag. 'That gold lattice will do nicely for starters.'

'The orb won't let you go near it,' said Jamie.

'We'll see about that,' said Krag. 'If *we* can't move that orb, trust me, no one can.'

'What about Worfeus?' Dregs whispered in Krag's ear. 'Perhaps he . . .'

Krag did not look pleased with that suggestion, but the children were keen to hear more, and so were the pets.

'I told you, his magic is no better than ours,' said Krag. 'Keep trying to get that lattice off, while we take a look at those bones.'

Once again, the children and pets were marched at wand-point to the house.

Jemima made a face at Jamie, and he knew what it meant. Their mum and Abigail's mum had gone to the market that afternoon and they were due back any minute. But there was little they could do to stop them walking in on a goblin invasion of their home.

The children and the pets followed Krag through the kitchen, down the hall and then they stopped outside the cellar door. It was locked with a new padlock Greg had bought, but with a swish of his wand, Krag broke it open. Several goblins hurried after him, then the children, Timber, Dougal, Trigger and Teddy were ushered down, followed by more goblins. Oberon flew down last and perched on top of a stack of crates. The rest of the animals and birds waited in the garden.

Gildevard was perched in a tall tree in the forest. Although bursting with curiosity, he knew it would be unwise to go any closer. He remained motionless, watching from a distance.

The foxes snuck over to the well, just in case anyone else decided to pay them a visit. The Brigadier and Sylvie sat beside the granite stone and kept an eye on the activities in the pond. But the goblins had no success. The orb avoided capture and continued to glow under the thickening ice.

The goblins with Krag swarmed into the cellar, and it wasn't long before they found the bones.

'Krool and Worb,' said Claw, handing Krag a couple of green, gnarled bones.

He smelled them, then threw them on the floor. 'That's them all right. Good riddance!'

Another goblin handed him a ledger.

'That belongs to our father now!' cried Jemima.

Krag glared at her and handed the ledger to the interrogator. He speed-read every page, shook his head and threw the book in the corner. 'Nothing of interest,' he muttered.

'I told you, bones and rubbish,' said Jamie, his face red with rage.

'Now what?' said Luke crossly.

Abigail glanced at Jemima, who immediately understood. The goblins' dark magic was making the boys angry. This could mean more trouble.

'Gold,' said Claw. '*Our* gold. It has to be here. Where have you hidden it?'

'We didn't find any gold,' cried Jamie.

'QUIET!' roared Krag. 'Keep looking,' he said to the goblins and they resumed their search.

'There's nothing here but rubbish,' said Claw as he kicked and tossed everything around. He was in no mood to do a proper search. 'While we're wasting time here, other hordes are going after the new gold mine.'

'If you say that one more time, I'll bind you with the vines!' roared Krag.

'Don't be so churlish,' said Dregs. 'We found the gold lattice, didn't we?'

'Oh, sure, we just can't get it off the orb,' said Claw.

A row broke out between those who wanted to stay and search for gold in Grindlewood, and those who wanted to head to the new gold mine before the best gold was taken. Soon there was so much noise, pushing and shoving that no one heard what was happening upstairs, except the pets.

Gloria and Esther had arrived home with several bags of herbs and funghi. Hearing the commotion, they left the shopping in the kitchen and hurried down the stairs to the cellar. They walked straight in to see the children, dogs, Teddy and Oberon watching a crowd of goblins having a heated argument.

Gloria stood in a state of shock, then let out a piercing scream. Esther whipped out a scented handkerchief from her pocket, waved it under Gloria's nose and whirled her friend out of the room and back upstairs as fast as she could. She ran to the kitchen and poured a sleeping draught into a mug, mixing it with some fairy lemonade she had left in the fridge the day before.

'Were they bob-blob-globglininins?' blubbered Gloria.

'Now, dear, you're just having a little fainting spell, a bad dream really.' Esther waved the hanky under Gloria's nose again, then she helped her to hold the mug. 'Drink this down and you'll feel better.'

The Swooning scent on the hanky dulled Gloria's senses enough to make her agreeable. She drank the potion and was soon in a deep sleep, propped up with several cushions on a kitchen chair. Esther hurried back to the cellar.

Gloria's high-pitched, out-of-tune-soprano scream had pierced the goblins' sensitive eardrums. Many of them roared with the sharp pain, as the scream seared through their heads long after Gloria had left.

Timber quickly spotted an opportunity. He threw back his head and let out the most raucous howl ever. It was a powerful sound, amplified greatly in the tightly-packed cellar. The other dogs followed suit and Teddy mewled as sharply as he could. Soon, every goblin was roaring, and then Oberon added his attack screech, the loudest one he knew, hovering over the goblins' heads to maximise the impact.

'We're leaving,' roared Krag, though he could hardly be heard above the din. 'But we'll be back,' he said, shaking his wand at Esther.

The goblin horde lifted their wands straight up in the air, while plugging one ear with their free hand. Moaning and wailing, they popped and were gone.

Out in the garden, the remaining goblins had heard the trouble and they disappeared quickly, back to their chambers.

The boys ran to the fairy house to help Jugjaw and Bushfire, who were still tied up, cursing and roaring. They were rolling around on the floor, trying to reach Jamie's sword so they could cut themselves free. Jamie grabbed it and cut the vines away and the dwarfs jumped to their feet.

'We're going to check on Hollow Hill,' said Bushfire. 'Tell Esther to send her nightingale to find Professor Allnutt.'

Jamie nodded and ran back to the kitchen.

Timber and the dogs hurried to the pond to check on the orb. It was still there, pulsing the same soft, amber light. The ice had thickened further and many of the reeds were frozen stiff. It wouldn't be long before the pond turned into a solid block of ice. No one would reach the orb then – unless the orb let them.

Chapter Sixteen

CONUNDRUMS

Esther explained how Gloria came to be in such a deep sleep – again.

'A scented hanky,' said Luke. 'Clever.'

'The Swooning scent is made from herbs and flowers rather than magic,' said Esther. 'Gloria will believe what she saw was only a dream.'

'Poor Mum,' said Jemima.

'Where's Granddad?' asked Abigail.

'He went to meet Peabody,' said Esther. 'I sent Nura to fetch him.'

'We have to check the cellar again,' said Luke. 'If the goblins think there's something down there, we need to find it first. We were lucky your mum's scream sent them packing.'

‘You’re right,’ said Jamie. ‘If the goblins find anything down there before we do they’ll think we were lying, or worse, that we’re the thieves.’

‘We should wait for Thaddeus,’ said Esther. ‘We’ll give it one hour, OK? Nura can find him quicker than anyone.’

Timber’s barking distracted everyone. The butterflies had arrived with yet another message, and it was a long one.

Beware and respect the lace of gold
Its strength is that of stranglehold.
Free the rain, and see the bow’s might,
How they will arc in coloured light.

Hearts so brave, so young and true
Must battle fiercely for the prize
That is not gold, nor power, nor might,
But sometimes comes at the highest price.

Timber ran off to tell the rest of the animals. They gathered by the pond, watching the water steadily ice over.

‘So the orb *is* dangerous,’ said Norville.

'The lattice has strength,' said Dougal. 'That's weird. I wonder how, exactly.'

'It protects the orb, so it must have magical power,' said Timber.

'What about the rain?' said Eldric, looking at the sky.

'And the bow,' said Cindy. 'Does it mean Luke's bow?'

'It's a riddle,' said Timber. 'Perhaps you could try to crack it, Eldric.'

The fox went into a huddle with his two sisters to try to figure it out.

'And the prize?' said Teddy. 'Does that mean the orb or something else?'

'It could be anything,' said Timber. 'So could the price. I wonder what that is.'

The children were asking a lot of the same questions.

'OK, we now know that the lattice is dangerous,' said Luke.

'The lace thing?' said Jamie.

'Nearly everything made from gold was made by goblins,' said Abigail.

'Dangerous,' repeated Luke.

'The Protection charms must be hidden in the lattice rather than the orb itself,' said Abigail.

'You mean booby traps?' said Jamie.

'Definitely dangerous,' said Luke.

'OK, I get it,' said Jamie. 'But we can't let anyone take the orb before the Wandeleis renew their magic, no matter what.'

They went over to the pond and stood beside the animals. The swans were sitting on the grass too, now that the ice was thickening. A slight glow was coming from the orb, though fainter than before. The four children and several of the pets bent low, watching it, wondering what to do.

Abigail thought of something. 'Maybe we should talk to it.'

'Are you *knowing* something again?' asked Jamie.

'I don't know,' said Abigail. 'I never know what I know, if you know what I mean.'

'Um, sure,' said Jamie. 'What'll we say?' He looked from one to the next.

Jemima thought of something. 'Why won't you let us move you somewhere safer?' she asked. 'We only want to help.'

Suddenly, the orb glowed brightly, then rolled

out from under the reeds.

'It's answering!' cried Jamie. 'Well done, Jem!'

The orb spun on the spot, throwing out beams of coloured light in a circle on the pond floor.

'What does that mean?' asked Jamie.

'It must trust us if it came out of hiding,' said Abigail.

'Maybe it recognised your magic, Jemima,' said Luke. 'I mean, a goblin gave your ancestor a wand, your wand, and goblins made the gold lattice. Maybe there's a connection.'

'Complicated,' said Jamie. 'Maybe it knows you're a true believer, Jem, and Timber is in the prophecy. Maybe the orb knows everything. Is that even possible?'

Before they could think about it, they heard Esther calling them inside. Thaddeus had arrived.

'We have to go now,' Jemima whispered to the orb. 'Keep yourself safe.'

The orb rolled back under the reeds, and the coloured light reduced to a glow. The children ran inside, followed by the dogs, Teddy and Oberon, who was keen to see his friend, Nura.

Once again, Gildevard flew off, unseen.

Thaddeus hadn't come alone. Peabody was standing

next to him, holding a pile of papers. Esther explained what had happened earlier with the goblins.

'How dreadful!' said Thaddeus. 'Thank goodness everyone is all right. I'm going to take another look down there now.'

Peabody was left in the kitchen with his papers, a mug of hot chocolate beside him, and a soundly-sleeping Gloria, still in her cushioned chair. Everyone else hurried down to the cellar.

'It's time to do an old-fashioned search,' said Thaddeus. 'Put on these gloves. Look, don't touch. Call me or Esther if you find anything, anything at all. Timber, dogs, Teddy, Oberon, be careful and make a noise if you find anything. Nura, you must wait upstairs with Peabody.'

Nura flew obediently back upstairs, and everyone got to work, feeling rather excited at what they might find. But there didn't seem to be much, other than crates of curtains and linen, broken things, torn things, the paintings, books and ledgers that had been found earlier. Thaddeus examined each bone carefully, feeling it, smelling it and using a small magnifying glass to look at every little detail.

'I don't think those bones should stay here any longer,' said Esther. 'Though if Krag returns and finds them gone, he might think we're up to something.'

'Or hiding something,' said Luke.

'You have a point,' said Thaddeus. 'I can't find anything to prove what really happened. It might be wiser to pack them up and leave them here. Jamie, Luke, gather the bones into this crate.' He pulled an empty wooden crate out from a corner.

'So the bones are safe?' said Luke.

'Yes,' said Thaddeus. 'They would have bewitched you the first time you found them if they had an Infinity curse. There's no sign of one. Any remaining magic could only be revived if very carefully cooked up in a cauldron.'

'Like the one Worfeus had in the forest?' asked Abigail.

'Exactly,' said Thaddeus. 'That cauldron was probably forged by the goblins too.'

'They make a lot of stuff, don't they?' said Jemima.

'They did. They were very skilled,' said Thaddeus. 'And some of them still are, but their greed for gold takes most of their time and attention now.'

'Sounds like the goblins' magic is stronger than

everyone else's,' said Luke. 'Sorry, Professor.'

'Some of it is,' said Thaddeus, 'but not all of it, and they certainly have different ideas about how to use it.'

The dogs and Teddy were scurrying around following even the faintest smell. Teddy began scratching at some debris. The dogs and Oberon joined him and they became very interested in it too. Timber barked for attention.

'They've found something,' said Jamie. He went over to take a look. It was difficult to make out what it was: finger-shaped, finger-sized, not perfectly formed, hard, black and heavy. 'What are these?'

'Lumps of . . . rat?' said Luke.

'Too heavy,' said Jamie.

'Rubble?' asked Esther.

'Don't think so,' said Thaddeus, peering through his magnifying glass.

'Timber, there's weird black stuff all over these finger-stick things,' said Teddy, 'but I think there's something underneath.' He scratched at it in a frenzy.

'Let me see,' said Timber. He tried to bite one.

'Timber, no!' cried Jamie. 'Down, boy. We don't know what that is.'

Oberon flew down and clawed at one, while Teddy scratched at another.

Then they all saw it: black varnish was scraping away, revealing a gold layer underneath.

'Oh my word!' cried Thaddeus. 'There is gold here! We have to know where it came from, and more urgently, was it payment for work, payment for a favour, or . . .' He looked at the children.

'Stolen,' said the boys.

'Hopefully not,' said Thaddeus.

'It must have been melted down and reshaped,' said Esther.

'And varnished black, all to hide it,' said Luke.

'But that doesn't mean George stole it,' said Jemima. 'He said in his diary that he worried about it. He might have tried to disguise it while he figured out what to do.'

'We must show that diary to Peabody,' said Thaddeus. 'Quick, everyone. Find every bit of this gold, I mean the black finger-shaped things, and pack them into another crate. Be careful you don't miss a piece.'

‘Here’s a good, strong crate,’ said Esther, dragging one over.

‘That’ll do nicely,’ said Thaddeus. ‘Timber and friends, I need you to sniff and scratch out the rest of it.’

The animals and Oberon got to work. Now they knew what they were looking for, they quickly sniffed out the varnished gold, which was scattered all over the cellar. It had been missed amongst all the rubble and rubbish. The children carefully began packing one crate with the gold and the other with the goblin bones.

‘I’m going up to Peabody,’ said Thaddeus. ‘Once everything is packed, cover the crates with those old rugs, and join us upstairs.’

Esther followed him out the door.

‘How will we explain this, Thaddeus?’ asked Esther. ‘The goblins will be furious. They’ll find out somehow.’

‘I know,’ said Thaddeus. ‘Let me think on it. Peabody has found something too.’

‘Will it prove George was innocent?’ asked Esther.

The children had been listening behind the door, but they couldn’t hear any more once Thaddeus and Esther went upstairs. Timber trotted over to Jamie and pawed at him. He had found something else, a letter.

When the children and pets came upstairs, Esther looked very worried as she listened to Thaddeus and Peabody arguing.

'Is that all you've got?' asked Thaddeus.

'I can't make up stories to prove George's innocence,' said Peabody, waving a scroll over his head. 'Everyone will know I'm lying.'

'Krag will claim that George is guilty, without *real* proof,' said Thaddeus. 'We need something more, something indisputable.'

'Maybe we should give the gold to Krag and apologise,' said Esther. 'The Grindles would be better off without it, and if we're lucky, it might send the goblins away.'

'Apologise!' cried Peabody. 'I don't think that would work.'

'What would you suggest?' asked Thaddeus crossly.

'Run,' said Peabody. 'Far, far away.'

Timber barked for attention as he trotted into the room with the others.

'Timber found this,' said Jamie, holding out the letter. 'We think it's in George's handwriting, but we're not sure what language it is.'

Thaddeus took the letter. 'It's goblin Gobbledegook,' he said. 'George couldn't possibly have learned that language, only goblins can. If this is his handwriting, then someone must have used a Translation spell to change it from English to Gobbledegook. But why?'

'This could be terribly important,' said Peabody.

'It could prove George's innocence,' said Esther.

'Or it could prove he's guilty,' said Peabody.

'Honestly, Herbie, try to say something hopeful once in a while,' said Thaddeus.

'I'm sorry,' said Peabody. 'Here's some more bad news: we can't translate Gobbledegook. Only goblins can.'

Chapter Seventeen

DISARRAY

Krag kept his prisoners waiting until the following morning.

'I saw the orb and the bones,' he bellowed.

'Excellent,' said Worfeus. 'Now, we'll take the orb, and you can have the lattice *and* the bones.'

'We also want our gold,' said Krag. 'And we haven't found it yet.'

'We didn't find it because it isn't there,' insisted Claw. 'We're just wasting time.'

'If you say that once more, I'll lock you up!' roared Krag, and he glared at Claw until he shook. 'We will discuss our plans in private, then I will give my orders.'

'You have no right to detain us any longer,' cried Zora. 'My gown is ruined, and my complexion must be suffering. You can keep Audmund and Vargon if you like, but I must return to the manor!'

'You will always look ugly to me,' muttered Krag, and he turned and walked away.

'Oh no!' cried Zora. 'I must look worse than I thought!'

'I warned you,' said Vargon. 'You drank too much of that Youth serum too quickly and now you've missed several doses. You'll be lucky if your whole recovery isn't reversed, along with your looks. More delays! More mistakes!'

Krag joined the waiting horde in an adjoining chamber. Discontented mutterings rumbled around the room. He listened for a minute as the goblins argued back and forth. 'Stop!' he roared. 'I am convinced the orb holds powerful magic. This mission will be worthwhile.'

'The orb did not respond to our spells, not even yours,' said Claw.

'Which tells us what?' said Krag.

Claw didn't dare say what he thought – that Krag's time as king was over.

'The bones belonged to Krool,' continued the king. 'He was a loner and a trouble-maker, but he was an exceptional goldsmith and magician. He must have known what was woven into that lattice, and that alone makes it worth having.' He looked slowly around the horde. 'I want that orb and the lattice in goblin hands – my hands, and not in the hands of those warring fools.'

'And the gold mine?' said Claw. 'We won't be able to stake a claim if we're late.'

'We can and we will,' said Krag. 'Half of you will go to the mine shortly, the rest of you will stay with me to finish this business and find out if the rumours of super-magic are true. Whatever is in that orb, I intend to take it *and* our gold.'

There were muted cheers from the crowd, but Claw and his friends weren't entirely satisfied.

'Release the prisoners,' said Krag. 'They're no threat to us, even if they think they are.'

'And the prophecy?' asked Rerm.

'I saw him,' said Krag. 'He's just a big dog.'

Krag frowned as the goblins dispersed. He had to succeed if he were to quell this unrest. Otherwise, his kingship might come to a fast and brutish end.

The prisoners were released with a spell and sent back to their own domains with a heavy bump. Arguments quickly followed in the manor.

'Why did you involve us with those goblins?' said Vargon. 'Look what they did to us. Are you afraid those children will outwit you again?'

'Nonsense,' said Worfeus. 'It's smarter to let the goblins and the warlocks deal with that goodie-two-shoes army, while we deal with what's important and leave with the real prize.'

'Is that what you thought the last time you faced them?' said Vargon.

'No one would expect children and their pets to have magic of any kind,' roared Worfeus. 'No one!'

'And what about your *superior* magic from Warlock Hell, eh?' said Vargon. 'Oh, I forgot, it's only some *inferior* type of magic after all. Bah!' He gulped down three goblets of vile, lumpy, brown brews that had been sitting on the parlour table for two days. His face turned green for a moment.

'I have always had superior magic,' said Worfeus, his eyes reddening. 'I was born with it and you'd do well to remember that.' He was reminded again of how Vargon had always favoured his sister over him. He was on the verge of firing his wand when Zora whirled into the parlour, having changed into a new gown.

'I'd like to keep that gold lattice for myself,' she said. 'It would make a nice shawl to accompany this gown. Or perhaps I could have it made into a veil. That would be very flattering.'

Vargon was too tired to argue about Zora's wardrobe again. Worfeus felt like exploding. He didn't want Zora annoying the goblins or making him look foolish. As he gazed around the room, trying to stay calm, his angry stare caused the furniture to wobble, and some of the cushions began to smoke.

Audmund closed his eyes and gripped the arms of his chair tightly, wondering how much longer he could keep his wits together.

'Why the cross face?' Zora asked her brother. 'Those goblins ruined my new dress, and I insist they pay for it with the lattice. Seems fair to me.'

'I promised the lattice to the goblins,' said Worfeus. 'And I will keep that promise so that Krag and his merry horde do as they are told.'

'I still think we could have finished this without involving goblins at all,' said Zora. 'When this is over, I will banish them from my kingdom forever.'

'*Our* kingdom,' said Worfeus. 'Listen to me, Zora, that horde will keep everyone busy while we take that wretched orb. Remember, we don't know how many will die trying to unlock its power, and I'd prefer if it wasn't me, I mean, us. I've been dead. It isn't pleasant!'

'You mean, you want to use them as cannon fodder?' said Zora.

'He means,' said Vargon, 'that we may need the goblins' special brand of dark magic to defeat the Wandeleis and the Grindlewood Army. How disappointing.'

'Yes, all right! You're both correct!' roared Worfeus. He hated to admit that the uncertainty surrounding the orb worried him, and that goblin magic might be needed to control it and win the battle. He glared at Vargon for exposing their weakness, then he turned to his sister. 'After we win, Zora, you may have all the dresses, shawls and veils that you desire.'

Zora sighed, then tried to glare at him, but she almost fainted.

'The dizzy spells will go if you get some rest and take your potions,' said Vargon. 'I'm going to bed. I advise you all to do the same. If we need the goblins to give us assistance, then we must be able to handle the goblins! Goodnight, everyone.'

'I'm going to check on my warriors,' said Worfeus.

'Are your poisonous pets in the forest ready?'

'Almost,' said Vargon, and he left the room.

Zora followed, then snuck off to the kitchen to whip up a Forbidden potion.

Worfeus whirled out the front door, around the side of the manor and over to the temporary barracks. After a few quick instructions to the warlocks on guard, he shunted off to the next dimension, hoping to return with more recruits. He would need more loyal warriors to keep Krag and his horde in check, as well as Zora and Vargon.

❧

Over in the garden, Edith, Evie and Elle arrived with yet another warning.

Before year end you must renew,
To make the magic strong and true,
But on the WABOM must be seen
The willow of the ancient queen.

If not this year, it must be soon,
Perhaps at springtime's fullest moon.
And when your magic's at its best,
'Tis then you'll face your greatest test.

‘They’re talking about the winter solstice and the first of spring,’ said Abigail.

‘Isn’t the first of spring in March?’ said Jamie. ‘How could we hold out till then?’

‘Just think, we could be wiped out before your twelfth birthday, Jamie,’ said Luke.

‘Not funny.’

‘Sorry.’

‘I think they mean February first,’ said Abigail. ‘February is the start of spring for magical people.’

‘Oh, right,’ said Jamie. ‘Better than having a battle near my birthday, I suppose.’

‘But we’re still hoping to be ready by December, aren’t we?’ asked Luke. ‘I mean, Jamie’s right. We couldn’t hold out till March, not without the Wandeleis’ magic.’

‘Their magic will be renewed as soon as the restoration is finished,’ said Jemima.

They looked at Abigail.

‘It’s down to the last few tiny pieces, on the last quarter page,’ she said. ‘I have to complete each symbol, one by one, then they have to dry. It takes time.’

‘I’m sure you’re doing your best,’ said Jemima.

'Come on,' said Jamie. 'We'd better let everyone know the latest message.'

Abigail took out the DimLock hanging around her neck and prepared to twist the top, when she stopped.

'What's the matter?' asked Jemima.

'We still have the four keys,' she said. 'The queen can't do the Renewal charm without this one.' She held up the crystal key which was hanging on the same string as the DimLock.

'Make sure you give it back to her,' said Jamie, 'or we'll be in more trouble.'

'We won't have it to protect us like we did before,' said Luke.

'But we can get it back after the ceremony, can't we?' asked Jemima. 'Maybe the other keys can do something too.'

'Luckily for us, you always see the best in everything,' said Jamie. '*And* we still have two gemstones.'

'But *only* two,' said Luke.

Jamie gave him a friendly frown. Just as Jemima saw the opportunity in everything, Luke saw the problem.

'Hey!' cried Abigail. The others stared at her. 'We could use one of the gems to translate the letter.'

'That's brilliant!' cried Jamie.

'Would it work on goblin magic?' asked Jemima.

'Good question,' said Abigail.

'We have to try it,' said Jamie.

'But if it doesn't work, the gem can't be used again,' said Luke.

'And if it does work?' said Jamie.

'Then we've only one gem left,' said Luke.

'But we'll know what's in the letter,' said Jemima.

'Granddad said it could be very important,' said Abigail.

'So is protecting ourselves and the pets,' said Luke.

'We have wands and spells,' said Jamie, pointing to the girls, 'and a sword, shield, arrows and bow.' He looked at Luke. 'And the magical people, and our brave pets.'

'*If* they renew their magic in time,' said Luke.

'I wish we could wish for a whole pouch full of gems,' said Jemima. 'Do you think we could use one to do that?'

'Brilliant!' said Jamie.

'Not allowed,' said Abigail.

'Yikes! This quest is the toughest yet,' said Luke.

It was hard to disagree.

Outside, the whole garden hushed when Gildevard flew down and landed on the grass. 'I was hoping we could do a deal,' he said.

'What do you mean, a deal?' asked Eldric.

'Explain yourself,' said Timber.

'I keep you informed about the manor and you allow me access to the orb,' said the eagle. 'I know you'll get to it first. You have it already, don't you?'

The animals and birds were aghast.

'The queen will decide what happens to the orb,' said Timber. 'You should tell us what's going on in the manor anyway.'

Gildevard stared at Timber with his beady eyes before replying. He wondered if Timber understood just how important he was to Grindlewood and all its magic. Perhaps the Wandeleis had not told him everything. 'Zora and Vargon have taken to their beds again,' he said reluctantly. 'A few days without potions in the goblin court has slowed them down. Worfeus doesn't need any potions, but he's worried. He's gone off to gather more troops. Audmund has locked himself away in his study. That's all I know.'

He departed before anyone made any comment. His visit only made the animals more agitated and Timber had to reassure them.

'It won't be long before the battle comes,' he said. 'The magical clans will be fighting for their kingdom, and we are caught up in the middle of their old feud. They each believe the orb can give them the edge in this battle, as well as afterwards. We need all the help we can get, even if that help comes from Gildevard. I'm going to the Eastern Woods with the children now. Keep watch, and keep ready. Teddy, you're in charge.'

Thaddeus met them at the edge of the woods, and Abigail told him about her gemstone idea. He brought them straight to the queen. Wanda had been practising with the willow again and looked utterly exhausted. The professors noticed her decline.

'Good heavens,' said Flint. 'We need Her Majesty strong and well.'

'She will be more powerful than ever if she can master that wand,' said Pendrick, trying to sound encouraging. 'Once she does, it will not drain her so much.'

'I'm afraid she will collapse and not be able to use it at all,' said Flint.

'We've talked about this before,' said Pendrick. 'There really is no other way. Worfeus and Zora will be very powerful if they unite. Only the willow can defeat them and only the queen can use it.'

'Worfeus and Zora were never on friendly terms before,' said Sparks. 'How have things changed?'

'They'll use each other to get what they want,' said Pendrick. 'It will be interesting to see what happens afterwards.' The other professors gasped. Afterwards? They weren't entirely sure who would emerge the winner.

When they gathered in front of the queen, Thaddeus explained about finding the gold and the letter, and Abigail's idea to use the gemstone.

'It might work,' said Pendrick.

'Very good, Abigail, very good,' said Sparks.

Flint nodded continuously as he thought about it.

'There aren't many ways of undoing goblin magic,' said Wanda, 'but the gemstone would be worth a try.'

'It would mean the children have only one gem left for the biggest battle in Grindlewood's history,' said Flint.

Pendrick frowned at him. 'Try not to scare everyone, Flint.'

'True,' said Wanda. 'Let me consider it for a moment.'

The queen and the professors sat in silence, while the children and Timber took a walk and watched the reindeer grazing in the woods. Whatever decision the queen made, they would have to abide by it.

'If the letter clears the Grindles of theft, then the goblins won't stick around,' said Pendrick. 'Not without a mutiny. That Claw fellow is very angry about being here, but any proof has to be clear enough for Krag not to challenge it.'

'What about the gold in the cellar?' asked Flint. 'Shouldn't it be given back?'

'To whom?' asked Thaddeus. 'If George is innocent, the gold belongs to his descendants.'

'And if he's guilty?' asked Sparks.

'The goblins probably believe the Grindles are guilty already,' muttered Flint.

'Enough, gentlemen, I have made my decision,' said the queen. 'Lotus, please call the children and Timber. If the gemstone has the power to translate this letter, let's hope we like what it reveals.'

Chapter Eighteen

TICK TOCK

Jemima opened the pouch and took out the next gemstone, the ruby. She passed it to her friend.

Abigail hesitated, suddenly wondering if she should have mentioned it at all.

'It's a good idea, Abi,' said Jamie, seeing the worried look on her face.

'We'll get the result we want,' said Jemima. 'Proof that George was innocent.'

'Hopefully,' whispered Flint.

Abigail held the ruby tight. Pendrick placed the letter in front of the queen, and they gathered close. Abigail closed her eyes and wished for the goblin's letter to be deciphered. Nothing happened.

'We've wasted it!' cried Luke.

'Calm down!' said Jamie crossly.

'The gems are powerful,' said Wanda. 'But this may take a while. Goblin magic is not easily overcome.'

The children looked at her. It was the first time she had admitted how powerful goblin magic could be, though they had begun to suspect it. There had to be a reason everyone was so worried about the goblins.

'If the letter proves George is guilty, we will feel the goblins wrath,' said Sparks. 'We must have the orb. We must!'

'I thought you didn't know what the orb can do,' said Luke.

'We don't,' muttered Flint. 'Not really.'

'We believe it is very special, very powerful,' said the queen.

'What about the willow wand?' said Jemima. 'Isn't that special too?'

'The willow is remarkable,' said Wanda. 'But it was enchanted by a crafty old goblin so it will not fight them willingly. Mastering it has been difficult, as you can see.'

They looked at her tired, lined face. She had aged greatly.

‘So, did the gem work? asked Jamie, looking impatiently at the letter.

‘The translation could take a day, a week, perhaps longer,’ said Pendrick. ‘I’ll keep it safe while we wait.’ He picked up the letter, folded it and put it inside his cape.

The children felt as glum as they looked. Timber whined at the queen.

‘Do not fret,’ said Wanda. ‘We have a little time. Zora and Vargon were unwell when we left the goblin court. They will not attack before they are ready, and Worfeus won’t risk an attack on his own. He’s a coward underneath all his bluster and showing off. The Worfagons are just as fearful of the orb as we are.’

‘Fearful?’ mumbled Luke. He glanced at Jamie, who was now looking very cross.

‘How can you be sure the Worfagons won’t surprise us?’ asked Jamie.

‘Timber heard they needed to recover from their ordeal,’ said Pendrick. ‘And Her Majesty is right – Worfeus won’t try to take the orb alone, not after his last visit to the garden.’

‘How do you know that, Timber?’ Jamie looked at his dog, and stroked his ears.

Timber gave a few muffled woofs that didn't mean much, which frustrated Jamie even more.

'The eagle told him,' said Wanda.

'Gildevard?' cried Jamie.

'The eagle could be lying,' said Luke. 'All the animals are very cross with him.'

'Especially Timber,' said Jamie.

'It was Timber who said so,' said the queen gently.

The children looked at one another, then at Timber again. He must believe what the eagle had said if he told the queen about it.

'Return to your lessons and practice sessions,' said Wanda. 'All of you, the animals too. If we're lucky, *The Book of Darkness* will be finished, the letter translated and telling us what we're hoping for, and the Renewal ceremony complete, all before the Worfagons attack.'

'But if just one of those events goes wrong, Your Majesty . . .' said Sparks.

'Excuse me, Your Majesty,' said Lotus. 'Timber has a visitor.'

Through the trees nearby, they could just make out the giant stag's antlers.

Timber bounded off to greet him. 'Sebastian, I was hoping to see you,' he said.

‘We should go over our plans,’ said the stag, ‘and I’d like you to meet the rest of the herd.’

The children hurried after Timber as he raced towards the reindeer. They were gathered in the centre of the woods.

‘We need to practise some of our manoeuvres,’ said the stag. ‘The reindeer are larger than the rest of your army and we don’t want any accidents during the battle.’

‘I’ll bring some of my team tomorrow,’ said Timber. ‘But the rest will have to stay behind on guard.’

‘That’s fine,’ said Sebastian. ‘Come, meet some of the reindeer now.’

The children stood watching as Sebastian introduced Timber to the herd. They sniffed each other’s scent, the reindeer rubbed their antlers on Timber, then they ran around for a while, showing Timber how to avoid their antlers. He also learned how to run with them without getting trampled on.

When they were finished with planning and practising, Timber ran back to the children, barking and wagging his tail. He wanted them to meet the reindeer too. The four children approached slowly, not wanting to startle the herd. They reached out and stroked the animals' necks and then their towering antlers, as the reindeer bowed their heads to confirm their friendship.

'They are so perfect,' said Jamie, gently petting one of the reindeer. 'And they love Timber.'

'Magnificent,' said Luke, stroking another. 'I've never seen reindeer this big.'

The girls wandered quietly through the herd, petting one reindeer after the next. The few quiet moments with the ancient herd had a soothing effect on all of them, so much so, they didn't realise just how long they had been there. Timber knew when it was time to go. He lifted his head and howled his happy howl.

'Timber's call,' said Jamie. 'Time for lessons.'

They left Timber with the stag and headed off to their classes with the wizards and witches: the boys to fencing, then archery, Jemima to spells and Abigail to *The Book of Darkness*. Everything was very nearly ready as the clock ticked down to the battle.

A week later, all the cats, dogs and foxes had visited the reindeer, and Abigail had finally finished her work restoring the pages. Another three days and the inks would be dry, the job done. Everyone in Hollow Hill breathed a sigh of relief. Then Abigail was called to see the queen.

'Your Majesty, I should have returned this earlier.' Abigail handed over the crystal key. 'I know you need it for the ceremony.'

'Thank you,' said Wanda. 'And I would like to give you this.' She handed her a beautifully decorated box, and inside, a set of restoration tools.

Abigail looked at her aunt, the queen, absolutely thrilled, but she could only whisper 'Thank you.'

'You're welcome,' said Wanda, smiling warmly. 'You have more than earned this gift. You have a wonderful talent, Abigail, and I can see it is your heart's desire to restore and renew old things, just as your Granddad told me some time ago.'

'He told you?'

'Yes,' said the queen. 'We can see this is what you love to do most of all. Your other lessons are important, but if restoration makes you happiest, then that is what you should choose.'

Abigail beamed with delight, relief at finishing her task, and the honour of receiving such a gift. Her thoughts turned to Pearl, but the queen had expected that.

'Pearl will need some time to recover, but the two of you will work side by side on many projects, I am sure of it,' she said. 'You will learn a lot from each other.'

❦

The Renewal ceremony took place at dawn on the winter solstice, the shortest day of the year and only four days before Christmas. This time, none of the Grindlewood Army was present. It was a quiet affair, overshadowed by the preparations for battle, scant as they were, and the need to keep it secret.

Later that morning, when the children had their final lessons in the Eastern Woods, Wanda offered them the crystal key. 'You may need this,' she said.

'I have that feeling too,' said Abigail. She put the key around her neck. 'What about the other keys?'

'Like the butterflies,' said the queen, 'the keys have their own magic, some of which we know and some we don't.'

Puzzled by the queen's words, the children returned home in silence. All of them felt nervous, knowing the battle was imminent and the odds were stacked against them.

Back in the fairy house, Jamie pulled the gold key out from under his sweater. 'I'd love to know what else this key can do.'

Luke took out the iron key, and Jemima the silver.

'So they're not just for the locks in the Pyramid Tomb,' said Luke.

'If they do have more magic, I'm sure they will help us,' said Jemima.

Holding their keys, they stood and looked out the crooked little window. Timber was in the garden going over the plans, including what they had practised with the reindeer over the previous few days. A strange calm fell on the garden and surrounding fields and forest. The wind held its breath, the clouds thickened then scudded across the sky. The temperature fell even further. Nature was waiting for the ultimate storm – the battle for the orb, the battle for Grindlewood.

Worfeus was frustrated. His latest band of warriors

didn't look at all battle-ready. Krag was avoiding him too and hadn't responded to his latest request to meet. The goblins remained in one of their labyrinths, keeping everyone guessing if, when and how many of them would join the Worfagon cause.

Zora was improving but she was still not fully restored. She had episodes of high energy, then moments of wilting and wailing. More and more potions seemed to be the only answer and she guzzled them greedily.

Audmund was nervously twitching, biting his nails, his silver eyes bulging bigger than ever. His private plan was shaky at best. He needed to get a grip on his nerves or he would fail spectacularly.

Vargon wasn't feeling any better, but he did his best to hide it. There was no way to undo all the shunting and dimension-hopping of recent months. All the dark magic he had used bringing Zora back from Oblivion had aged him rapidly. As each of the Worfagon allies tried to deal with their own problems and secret plans, arguments continued to rage in the manor.

'Don't you dare begin this battle without me!' cried Zora. 'I need a few more days, that's all, then I'll be ready to destroy that queen.'

'We should attack before the Wandeleis renew their magic,' said Audmund. 'Why can't everyone see that?'

'What makes you think we need your advice?' asked Worfeus.

'I know how they do things,' said Audmund. 'I was one of them, remember? And I've been very useful around here, especially to you.' He risked a glare at Worfeus.

'It's hard to be patient when we're so close,' said Vargon, 'but there's no doubting our superiority. A few days won't matter. My spiders need a bit more time anyway. By the way, I gave Grizzle some of their medicine; it should give him an extra edge.'

'He didn't need an extra edge,' muttered Audmund, rolling his eyes. Giving a dwarf-troll medicine of any sort was risky. But arguing was useless at this point. Vargon and Zora went to Vargon's study to drink another collection of potions. Worfeus went outside for some air. He had big plans for ruling his new kingdom, especially with the power the orb would give him. That and all his power from Warlock Hell, despite what the goblin king thought.

'I will prove that I am the greatest warlock of all time,' he thought. 'And soon, I will be the greatest king. The two queens can fight it out, and if they don't destroy each other, I'll step in and finish them both off. Ha! Their followers will scatter and my army will crush them. I will easily dispense with old Vargon and the traitor, and Krag won't care once he gets his gold. No one can reach the orb without removing the lattice – and to do that, we need the gold key – something I found out in Warlock Hell. Ha! I'll bet no one else knows about that. Ha ha!'

The warlock's expression changed suddenly from excitement to fury. 'Those children and animals embarrassed me before but they will not do it again. I will destroy that garden and suck Grindlewood into my realm. Yes! MY realm! At last, Grindlewood, the very heart of the magical world, will be mine – FOREVER!'

Chapter Nineteen

BATTLE BEGINS

Thursday, December twenty-first dawned cold and grey. Heavy clouds sat low over Grindlewood, ominous and unmoving.

After the Renewal ceremony, Wanda tried to encourage her clan, but she had to include some words of warning. 'The orb must not fall into enemy hands,' she said. 'We must do whatever it takes to . . .'

Then she collapsed.

'Oh, disaster!' said Sparks, raising his hands to his mouth too late to muffle his outburst.

'Professor, please!' said Pendrick. 'We mustn't start a panic right before the battle.'

'Her Majesty is the only one who can use the willow,' whispered Sparks. 'Nothing else can match the power of Worfeus and Zora.'

'Two of them but only one Wanda,' added Flint.

'Gentlemen, no more negative thoughts,' said Pendrick. 'The fairies will take care of the queen, and she will join us as soon as she recovers. The rest of us must go to the garden immediately.'

When they arrived, the professors took up their positions. Sparks and Flint went to opposite ends of the garden with their teams. Pendrick led his wizards to a spot close to the well and the fairy house. Thaddeus remained near the main house with Esther, Tamara and the other healing witches who all carried rucksacks filled with potions and tinctures.

The children were organising their weapons behind the upturned rowing boat; it would provide some cover from incoming spells. Jamie tested Gorlan's sword in his right hand while holding Gorlan's shield in his left. They felt strong and inspiring, and he felt confident after all his practice. Luke tested his bow; the string was just right. He checked the quivers, one filled with silver arrows, the other with gold. The girls each wore another quiver over their shoulders with extra arrows provided by the archery wizards. Luke loaded a silver arrow and checked his aim.

Jemima and Abigail raised their wands. Both girls had excelled in their final lessons, differently though equally skilled. Abigail was careful and accurate, Jemima, courageous and quick.

'The diamond is in here,' said Jemima. She patted the pocket that held the last gemstone. Each of the children had their key. They knew the crystal key could produce a protective shield if they needed to call on it. The other keys were still a mystery.

Sebastian Stag and the reindeer had arrived during the night.

'We are very grateful for your help,' said Timber.

'And we are honoured to help the *worthy*,' replied the stag.

The herd bowed from where they stood in amongst the cluster of chestnut trees at the end of the garden. All the pets were relieved to see them, but Teddy frowned. He knew that if anything happened to the stag, Timber had promised to replace him. That would mean leaving Grindlewood and the Grindles forever, and leaving Teddy too.

'Don't worry about what might or might not happen,' said Timber, sidling up to his best friend. 'We have a job to do and we mustn't think of anything else.'

'Is Ernie OK?' asked Teddy, trying to distract himself and not think of how he might lose Timber.

'He's a little glum,' said Timber, 'but I think he understands why it's too dangerous for him to be involved this time.'

'If he can't heal goblin magic, then it's better he stays safe,' said Teddy.

'Esther and Tamara will look after the healing duties,' said Timber.

'I hope we don't need them too much,' muttered Teddy.

He reached up and rubbed his face against Timber's cheek as the big dog reached down to give him a lick.

Suddenly, they heard commotion in the field behind the garden. Some of the goblins had arrived.

'Here they come,' barked Timber.

Worfeus shunted into the forest with his unruly band of warlocks and a scattering of warwitches – fierce-looking hags, more horrid even than the Crabbage crones. He marched through the trees, then across the field towards the garden, confident and smug, at the head of the Worfagon army.

Zora whirled in next, surrounded by hundreds of enormous, venomous bats. They fluttered around her like a massive dark cloak. She wore a blood-red gown for the occasion, covered with ruffles and flounces that flopped about her neck, wrists and ankles. She strode proudly beside Worfeus, not wanting to be outdone by her twin brother.

Vargon and Audmund had not been included in Worfeus and Zora's grand entrance. They remained on higher ground, the metal hawks hovering above them. Using a spyglass, Vargon carefully surveyed the scene below.

'Those warlocks were useless in Bodric's Gorge,' said Audmund.

'They weren't much use in the manor last spring either,' said Vargon. 'But Worfeus managed to recruit a lot of them and they should keep the Wandeleis occupied for a while at least.'

'What about the goblins?' asked Audmund. 'We won't be able to control them, despite what Worfeus says. They barely take orders from their own king.'

'I agree,' said Vargon. 'But we'll let Worfeus worry about that.' He lowered the spyglass. 'Send the hawks down once the spell-fire intensifies. I'm going back to the manor.'

'What?' cried Audmund.

'I won't be long,' said Vargon, sneering at his nervous ally. 'My two prime spiders need their final dose of Rage potion, and so does Grizzle.'

Audmund grimaced.

'What's the matter now?' asked Vargon crossly. 'Just keep an eye on things. You can do that, can't you?' Vargon pressed his onyx ring and vanished.

More goblins emerged from secret tunnels that were dotted around the surrounding fields. There weren't as many as Krag had originally promised because some had been sent to the mine. Worfeus was annoyed.

'Krag hasn't kept his side of your bargain, has he?' said Zora. 'Looks like you might have to do some of the dirty work after all.'

'And that's what you're dressed for, is it?' said Worfeus.

His sister glowered at him. 'I'm here to finish Wanda in style. *You* can deal with the other nonsense.'

'I already defeated that witch,' said Worfeus. 'I will watch your efforts with interest.' Then he ordered the attack, drowning out his sister's angry retorts. 'Warlocks and warwitches to BAAATTTTLE!'

The field behind the garden exploded with wand-fire as the two magical clans fought fiercely, and the dwarfs took on the goblins. Worfeus and Zora kept out of the fighting and were pleasantly surprised as the Worfagon warriors advanced steadily. It wouldn't be long before the fighting reached the garden.

Flint and Sparks moved their teams to the garden wall. After climbing to the top, they fired down on the battle below. The warlocks were taken by surprise, but the goblins split into groups; some remained to fight the dwarfs, others turned and targeted the garden wall. They cast so many spells, and at such a fast rate, that the professors and wizards had to retreat. Though reluctant to be there at all, the goblins wanted to finish the job quickly. They were sharp duellers and their magic was deadly. Worfeus was impressed.

The dwarfs were so busy deflecting spells, they had no time to do their famous acrobatics that had worked so well in previous battles. On top of that, Audmund had sent in the hawks, and they were now attacking everyone from above.

Injuries began to mount. Esther sent Tamara and half the healing witches out through the gap in the garden hedge and across the back field to reach the wounded. The rest of Esther's team waited in the garden, knowing that trouble and injuries would not be long in coming there too.

Timber instructed the birds to form a perimeter around the garden. They were to watch for any surprise attacks, and to sound the alarm if any hawks or bats tried to veer off and surprise them. Leaving Oberon in charge of the skies, Timber and Sebastian organised the animals. They broke into groups just as they had rehearsed.

The dogs growled and howled, the cats hissed, the foxes barked. Norville rattled his prickles, but only from inside the kennel. Timber had asked him to stay out of the battle, much to the hedgehog's relief. Ramona and her friends had insisted on taking part and now hundreds of rabbits were flexing their kick-boxing muscles. They would work in large groups to thump any injured bats or hawks out of the garden. The rest of the time, they were to hide in the bushes, bouncing out to surprise the enemy.

Worfeus grew more excited, but also more impatient. He ordered the warlocks over the garden wall, leaving the field to the goblins. Krag glared at him. He didn't want his horde being drawn into a long battle in the field, far from the pond where the orb was waiting. He also knew that any gold would be in or near the house and that's where he wanted to be – close to the gold and close to the orb. Realising that a revolt might occur any moment, Krag reversed Worfeus' command and ordered the horde into the garden.

Worfeus and Zora marched proudly on, ignoring what was happening behind them, and deflecting a spell or two with a deft flick of their wands. They didn't care about anyone else's plans now; they had their own – their stated plan and their private ones too.

'Advance!' screeched Zora. The bats left her and soared over the chestnut trees. They plummeted down into the garden where several were speared by the waiting reindeer's antlers. Worfeus and Zora floated up and over the trees and landed on the far side of the pond, out of harm's way and in a perfect position to survey the action.

The conflicting battle plans were adding to the chaos, with Krag, Zora and Worfeus all giving different instructions to their troops. Soon the garden was ablaze with wand-fire, lightning flashes and firework sizzles.

There was the occasional explosion too, followed by puffs of smoke and a cacophony of animal noises, dwarf roars and goblin cries.

The professors looked to each other for inspiration. They needed a better plan, and quickly, but there was still no sign of Wanda.

As the number of injured grew, Esther darted around the garden, followed by the other healing witches. To reach the wounded, they had to dodge swords and arrows, duck past duels, deflect spells, and try to avoid the flocks of attacking bats and hawks.

The dwarfs had a bad history with the goblins. They looked angrier than ever as they charged into each fight, using all the weaponry they had – wands, hammers, pickaxes, fists and even teeth. The goblins' superior spell-speed and magic skills took a heavy toll, and like the professors, the dwarfs urgently needed a better plan.

Bushfire had brought Ripley along to witness the battle, hoping to teach him a lesson. 'Just look at all this mayhem, Ripley! You're partly to blame for this too, you stupid spy!' He hung the wicker cage from one of the apple trees. 'Now, you sit up there and watch!'

The squirrel trembled and twitched, stuck in the

tree, swinging in his cage. He barely dared to look at the fighting all around him. Several spells scorched his cage and his fur. He almost fainted as he watched Timber launch himself at a couple of warlocks, all the while trying to dodge a squadron of metal hawks. Timber was cut and bitten, only recovering and returning to the action after Esther reached him and healed his wounds.

Over near the beehive, Sparks prepared to try a new spell. When they were ready, his team barged their way to the centre of the garden and together they cast a Sweeping spell. Sinking low to the ground, they swung in a circular motion. 'Liquidicutius!' they cried.

With a bit of luck, the new spell would undo Vargon's Advanced Metal spell, the one that gave the hawks a tough metal coat. It worked. Every hawk within range began to melt. As the liquefied metal stuck to their wings, they fell to the ground, twisted and mangled, only to be thumped out of sight by dozens of boxing rabbits. Full of excitement, some of the bunnies looked around for something else to thump, but Ramona called her team back under cover to wait for the right moment.

Jemima and Abigail used Jelly spells to slow down the warlocks, allowing the Wandelei wizards and witches to overpower them with more advanced magic. It had worked well in previous encounters, but didn't have the same effect when they tried the spell on the goblins.

'What's wrong?' cried Jemima, as she ducked behind the rowing boat to avoid an incoming spell.

'Goblin magic,' said Abigail. 'We might have to leave them to the dwarfs for the moment.'

'The dwarfs are having a tough time,' said Luke.

'The goblins make a big difference, don't they?' said Jemima. 'I didn't realise their magic was so, so –'

'Dark and powerful?' said Abigail.

Jemima looked at her. 'Will we be able to stop them?'

'We have to,' said Abigail. 'Otherwise . . .'

'The animals are being destroyed,' yelled Jamie, tucking in beside them. 'Esther is healing them, but they're being hurt so many times. Give me the diamond, Jemima. We have to use it.'

Jemima fumbled in her pocket and took out the pouch.

'Wait! It's our last one!' cried Luke, as he fired off

three arrows instead of two. 'Can't the witches heal them?' he asked, catching the returning arrows after they had hit all three targets. He stuffed them into the quiver on his back.

'I told you, they already are,' cried Jamie. 'But they won't always get to them in time.'

'Then ask Timber,' said Luke. 'Ask him if we should use it.'

Jamie was surprised by that remark, but Timber was right beside him. Jamie held his collar and looked at him.

'I want to use the diamond to protect you and the pets,' he said. But Timber reacted with a growl and took up a pounce position.

'You see?' said Luke. 'He doesn't like the idea.'

'He's too brave,' said Jamie. 'He'll want us to keep the last gemstone for ourselves.'

Timber barked his 'yes' bark and ran back to the dogs who were trying to pull a warlock off one of the dwarfs.

'OK, so you're both right,' said Jemima. 'What now?'

'I know we're going to need it, Jamie, but I don't think it's the right time,' said Abigail.

Jemima put the pouch away.

'All right, then,' said Jamie. 'What about the crystal key?'

'Better idea,' said Luke, as he fired more arrows.

'Everyone under its protection has to be holding it, all the time, and we have to hold the animals too,' said Abigail.

'I forgot!' cried Jamie. 'It's so awkward.' He turned and slashed the wands of two advancing warlocks. They were stunned for a moment, then Jemima and Abigail followed up with Wobble spells that put them out of action until Thaddeus finished them off.

Three bulky warlocks were closing in from the side. Jamie turned just in time to block a downward sword swipe with his shield, then engaged one warlock in a sword fight. As Timber returned to help, he lunged in from the side, knocking another warlock away from the girls, but a third one thrust his sword at Luke, sending him flying backwards.

'NO!' cried Jamie and he hurried back to his friend. Bushfire, Jugjaw and the cats and foxes rounded on the two warlocks as the children tried to help Luke.

'Let me in there,' cried Thaddeus.

Leaving the dwarfs to duel, the animals took up

guard positions. The Worfagon sword was sticking out of Luke's chest. Everyone was afraid to touch it, though strangely, there was no blood.

Luke opened his eyes. 'Huh, what?'

'You bumped your head when you fell backwards,' said Thaddeus, as calmly as he could.

'Aaaaggghhhhh!' cried Luke, suddenly seeing the sword.

'Don't touch it,' said Thaddeus. 'I'm going to take a look.' Carefully, he felt Luke's chest, pulled the iron key out from under his sweater, then removed the weapon. 'The tip of the sword stuck in this!' said Thaddeus, holding up the key.

'Lucky Luke,' said Jamie, and he gave his friend a puck in the shoulder. 'Come on, back to work!' He helped Luke to his feet.

'Thank goodness,' said Thaddeus, mopping his brow. 'Be careful, all of you.'

'Thanks, Professor,' said Luke, rubbing his chest. He hung the key around his neck again. 'I guess we have more magic than I thought.'

Jamie smiled, then shouted, 'Duck!' as he slashed at some incoming bats.

'Don't get bitten!' cried Thaddeus, turning to

face a nasty-looking warwitch.

The battle raged on, though Worfeus and Zora stayed largely out of it, preferring to watch from the far side of the pond. Zora was saving her energy for the duel with Wanda. Worfeus intended only to tidy up any remaining threats at the end, though that looked to be a long way off yet. A few disgruntled goblins were sitting high up in trees, refusing to get involved. Gildevard was perched near them, watching too.

Sebastian Stag sent half his herd through the gap in the hedge to the field behind the garden. They charged, using their antlers to gore any warlocks who were still out there. One or two reindeer fell foul of repeated bat bites, but most escaped trouble and returned to the garden once the back field was cleared. They ignored the wounded Worfagon warriors who were scurrying away to the nearest portal.

Jamie felt for the gold key hanging around his neck under his sweater. It felt warm, something he hadn't noticed before. After seeing what happened to Luke, the girls checked their keys too. The silver key swung around Jemima's neck as she cast spell after spell at every target near her. But after a hard tumble to avoid a goblin spell, the key popped out from under her coat. And it was lucky that it did.

Vargon's enhanced bats began to notice a pattern in the girls' spells and they came up with a counter plan. Six of them veered off from the main group and zoomed towards Jemima. Teddy raced over but couldn't outrun them, his hissing and meowing drowned out by all the noise. But Cindy and Sylvie heard him, and so did Timber. They followed quickly.

The bats closed in, their mouths wide open. They were ready to bite when Abigail saw them too. 'Jemima, look out!'

Jemima swung around. The bats were almost in her face, when they buckled and balked, blinded by a sudden flash from the swinging silver key around her neck. Several flew into each other, others flew straight into the ground, and all were destroyed by the arriving pets, sharp shooting from Luke and sword swipes from Jamie.

'Saved by another key!' cried Jamie, but his own key was beginning to bother him. It was so hot now it was burning him through his clothes. And something else was odd.

'Jamie!' cried Luke.

'What?'

'Look.'

Jamie looked towards the frozen pond. It was all lit up and getting brighter and brighter. There was a noise coming from it too, a kind of whining. Soon the glare was so intense from both the ice and the orb's light, everyone had to cover their eyes and most of the fighting stopped, except for a few duels further away from the pond.

Krag marched to the edge of the water, shielding his eyes. Worfeus was already moving quickly around from the other side of the pond, taking care not to look directly at the light and not wanting to float over the water just in case the orb reacted. Zora hurried after him, tripping repeatedly in her voluminous gown. She wore a curious eye mask that protected her from the glare.

'You came prepared for bright lights,' said Worfeus. 'Were you expecting a photographer?'

'It's a fashion piece, a touch of drama to go with my gown,' said Zora. 'I bet you wished you had one now.'

The light had softened a little by the time Worfeus joined Krag and peered into the pond.

'The orb is in there and using its magic,' said Worfeus, a twisted smile spreading across his face.

'Tell the goblins to get it,' said Zora. 'That's what they're here for.'

Krag turned and glared at her.

'The orb froze that pond,' said Jamie, marching up to Krag, Worfeus and Zora. 'No one can get it out unless it wants to come out, not even one of you.'

'Is that so?' said Worfeus.

'Stand back, all of you,' said Krag. He raised his wand and cast several spells but the ice remained solid. 'That's ridiculous!'

'Let me at it,' said Worfeus, muscling in front of him. But he too failed to break the ice.

'My turn,' said Zora smugly, but she managed only to burn the flounces on the hem of her gown.

Everyone looked at the royals, bewildered. What sort of magic could resist all three of them?

Chapter Twenty

PROOF

Completely ignoring his sister, Worfeus turned to the goblin king. 'Together,' he said.

Krag nodded. 'Three, two . . .'

'One!' cried Worfeus, and they fired.

Zora immediately saw a new problem: an alliance between her brother and Krag was the last thing she wanted. As she watched the spells burn into the ice, she knew she would have to be careful or the orb might be snatched by one or both of them, possibly while she was busy duelling with Wanda. 'Never mind,' she thought, after a brief moment of doubt. 'I'm smarter than those two put together. It won't take me long to defeat the little queen and I'll do it in front of her clan. Then I'll command their loyalty and demand the orb.'

She pushed the problem of Worfeus and Krag from her mind. 'Where is that wretched queen anyway?' She scanned the crowd. No sign.

Zora frowned as her brother and Krag shouted excitedly. Little cracks started to appear in the ice. Suddenly there was a thunderous crunch as the ice split deeply, zig-zagging down the length of the pond. Worfeus and Krag lowered their wands. Everyone moved cautiously closer, and closer still, till there was a large crowd staring into the pond, including the children and the pets.

Krag spotted Timber. He had read up on the Ancients' prophecy and wouldn't be dismissing the big dog as quickly as he had before. Timber's resemblance to the wolf Tyrus was striking, and it put Krag on edge. Timber growled at him.

'Call your dog off,' roared Krag.

'You keep away from him!' yelled Jamie.

'Your family should keep away from what is mine!' cried Krag.

'How many times do we have to tell you, we didn't take your gold,' cried Jemima. 'How could we? That was a century ago.'

'You, your ancestors, you're one and the same,' shouted Krag.

Worfeus sniggered. It was easy to make the goblins cranky, it was one of their big weaknesses, that and greed. The greater their irritation, the more they would be distracted from what he suspected was their true goal – the gold *and* the orb.

Timber looked ready to lunge.

'Leave the dog, Krag,' said Claw. 'Harming him might bring a curse upon us.'

Krag turned slowly and glared at Claw. 'I'm aware of that, you idiot. That's why I kidnapped their father.' He turned back to the children with a gloating smile.

'Wha-aat?' cried Jemima.

'NO!' cried Jamie.

'Oh, surely not,' whispered Pendrick.

'He should be in my goblin court by now,' said Krag, 'all tied up and TERRIFIED!'

Timber barked very loudly, and both Jamie and Luke had to hold him back.

'Don't any of you try spells or tricks on me,' said Krag, 'or the kiddies' daddy will be hanged. Now, call that dog off and lower your wands!'

Jamie persuaded Timber to stand down. He lined up with the other dogs, cats and foxes, all of them furious.

'You took our dad?' screamed Jemima. But instead of dissolving into tears, she pointed her wand at the goblin king and fired every spell she could think of as she walked towards him. Krag deflected each one with ease, but it annoyed him to have to deal with a girl who shouldn't have magic at all.

'How can you do spells?' he roared. 'You're not a witch! Horde, deal with her. I've got more important things to do.'

Claw and his gang stepped forward, grumbling. As the goblins reluctantly blocked Jemima's spells, Abigail joined in beside her, then Thaddeus, then Pendrick. Soon spells were flying back and forth, everyone taking the magic up a notch, till it was just as intense as before.

Flint, Sparks and their teams of senior wizards began duelling again as more goblins were drawn in alongside Claw and his mates. Jamie used his shield to block spells as the girls were forced to retreat, then everyone stopped again when another thundering crack came from the pond. The whining grew louder.

Krag and Worfeus returned to blasting the ice.

'Krag is lying,' Thaddeus said quietly to the children. 'My wizard friends are keeping a close eye on your parents. Your father's at the mill, like I arranged, and your mother is with a friend of Esther's, making herbal teas.'

'Are your wizards able to deal with these goblins?' asked Jamie. 'Because I don't think we're doing so well.'

'Yes they are, and we're doing just fine,' said Thaddeus. 'Goblins tell lies all the time and they won't put up with this nonsense for much longer. Trust me, your father is safe, but for goodness' sake, don't let Timber near Krag.'

'Any message from Peabody?' asked Pendrick, arriving beside them, his cape in tatters.

'Nothing yet,' said Thaddeus.

'What's Peabody up to?' asked Jamie.

'Is he with Dad?' asked Jemima.

'No,' said Pendrick. 'He's watching the letter. I gave it to him earlier in case it translates while we're busy.'

The children didn't feel at all relieved. But just at that moment, Peabody ran into the garden looking for Thaddeus. Esther saw him and pointed him in the right direction.

Worfeus was now roaring with excitement, while Krag stood quietly, staring into the water. The goblins were beginning to find the whining noise unbearable.

'It worked!' said Peabody, waving excitedly.

'Over here. Quick!' said Thaddeus. He pulled Peabody behind the rowing boat.

'George didn't steal anything,' said Peabody.

'Thank the Ancients!' muttered Thaddeus. 'Do you have proof?'

Peabody took the letter and a small scroll out of his tunic. He handed them to the professor. 'The information in the letter helped me find that scroll amongst all of George's other papers, the stuff Greg was sorting through,' he said. 'It is absolute proof that George made a perfectly good business deal, which was paid for in gold, and it had no connection with the goblins' lost gold.'

Thaddeus read both documents. 'The scroll is the contract showing the business deal, the payment, where it came from and from whom, yes, yes.' He read on. 'The letter mentions all the details about how a goblin – Krool – gave George's sister a touch of magic in exchange for gold, which she took from the cellar, but it was the same gold that George had received for the business he did, and *not* any stolen gold.' Thaddeus didn't read all of it out loud, but skipped to the important bits. 'George suspected he was being followed by someone – that was probably Worb – the same goblin who followed Krool and confronted him as he was trying to steal the rest of the gold from the cellar. My, my.'

'I think Krool intended to leave a false trail back to George to avoid being discovered himself,' said Peabody.

'What a villain!' said Thaddeus.

The children scurried over.

'Well?' said Jamie, crouching beside the two wizards.

'George is innocent,' said Thaddeus. 'We have to show this to Krag.'

'Will the goblins leave now?' asked Jemima.

'At least some of them will,' said Thaddeus. 'Krag still wants the lattice, and maybe the orb too, but his horde might have other ideas. Come along, Peabody, let's find out.'

Peabody stood up and his hat was immediately destroyed by a Fire spell. 'Merlin's beard!' he cried and slumped down again. While everyone was distracted by what might happen in the pond, the dwarfs had launched a surprise attack on the goblins sitting in the trees, and spell-fire was coming from high and low.

'Stay behind me,' said Thaddeus. 'Girls, Luke, some blocking spells and arrows, please. Jamie, your shield!'

Jamie held Gorlan's shield out in front while the girls and Luke fired from behind, trying to open a safe passageway to the goblin king. Timber trotted beside Jamie. He wasn't letting any of the children approach the goblin king without him.

'Krag!' called Thaddeus.

The goblin king didn't even look up.

'KRAG!' roared Jamie, and Timber barked.

'I told you to keep that dog away from me,' said Krag, glowering at them.

'We have proof,' cried Thaddeus, making sure all the goblins nearby would hear. 'We have proof that the Grindles didn't take your gold. This is not your battle, Krag. You won't find any of your lost gold here. The Worfagons lied to you.'

Krag's face burned with anger. He knew the

horde would be furious to know they had been fooled. Claw was already spreading the word. This could mean mutiny.

The goblin king held up his wand and shot a spell into the sky. Thunder rumbled overhead and everyone's magic temporarily froze. All turned to the furious, red-faced king. 'Let me see this proof!' he roared. 'Who was the thief? Show me!'

'It doesn't say *who* robbed you, but it does prove it wasn't the Grindles,' said Peabody nervously. 'Any gold they earned or inherited is rightfully theirs.'

Krag snatched the letter and read it. Claw, Dregs and several other goblins crowded around. George had written the account in English, but Krool had to use a spell to translate it into Gobbledegook in order to read it. It was now back in English again, and Krag could read both languages. When he was finished, he bit into the paper with his dirty teeth.

'Is it a fake or not?' asked Claw.

The smell and the sharp taste of nettle left no doubt.

'It's real,' said Krag. He threw the letter on the ground.

'Do you wish to read the scroll as well?' asked

Peabody, gingerly holding it out.

'No,' said Krag. 'I want the lattice for my trouble.'

Krag turned away and sat down at the edge of the pond. All he could do now was wait for the lattice, and if he was lucky, the orb. Without some compensation, his horde would surely desert him.

Worfeus was having similar thoughts. As soon as the orb was out of the pond, he wanted to give Krag the lattice and be rid of him and his horde. To do that, Worfeus had to find the gold key and remove the lattice from the orb, though he suspected that wouldn't be as easy as it sounded. 'Enough of this nonsense,' he roared. 'Someone has the gold key, the one that opens the lattice. Which of you has it?' Worfeus pointed a long, hook-nailed finger at the children one by one, then walked slowly towards them. 'It has to be one of you. Give it to me NOW.'

'Jemumble has the silver one,' said Zora. 'I saw it around her neck.'

'Her name's Jemima,' said Jamie defiantly.

'I want the *gold* key,' said Worfeus. 'I don't care about any silver.'

No one spoke for a moment, as they watched Worfeus pacing up and down. Timber growled and looked ready to pounce again, causing Worfeus to hesitate. He looked as uncomfortable about being near the dog as Krag did. Worfeus' patience finally ran out. 'Warlocks, get me that key!' he roared.

Several Wandelei wizards rushed forward to surround the children, but only a few reluctant warlocks obeyed Worfeus, and trudged forward. All eyes turned towards the pond when the ice suddenly exploded into thousands of fragments. The orb bobbed to the surface, beaming colourful rays of light around the garden. The whining noise changed to an excited whirr.

'What is that?' asked Jamie.

'I think it's crying,' said Jemima.

'It can float,' said Luke.

'Indeed,' thought Worfeus. 'This is special magic.'

'I knew it,' thought Krag. 'There's more to that orb than anyone knows or understands. See how that lattice shines!'

Zora looked from one to the other, frowning. There were far too many people interested in this orb, her orb. And where were Vargon and Audmund? She looked around but didn't see either of them.

The orb bobbed in the broken ice. Timber's growls grew louder as worrying thoughts went round in his head. 'You will know what to do, when the time comes,' Wanda had told him. He hoped the queen was right, because he could feel the orb calling to him, and he would have to answer it soon.

Chapter Twenty-one

SPIDER SHOCK

When Vargon returned to the garden, he was dismayed by what he saw. 'Why is everyone standing around?' he cried.

'Krag temporarily froze all magic so he could read a letter,' said Worfeus. He glared at the goblin king.

'That numpty goblin! Where's the orb?' roared Vargon.

'It's in the pond,' said Worfeus, 'merrily beaming out rays of coloured light and making a hideous whine.'

'Go and get it!' cried Vargon. 'This is our chance to get the orb and destroy the Wandeleis. Make sure your army is ready once the magic resumes.'

'Be quiet!' roared Krag. 'We watch and wait.'

Vargon looked at him, perplexed. 'Is this what you call giving assistance?' Then he turned to Zora. 'What about Wanda?'

'She hasn't arrived yet,' said Zora in a bored voice.

'We can deal with the orb and Wanda,' said Worfeus. 'You may go, Vargon.'

Vargon glared at him. 'This battle should be over by now. Where is Audmund?' He looked urgently left and right.

'Who cares?' said Zora.

'We have everything under control,' said Worfeus. 'Why don't you crawl back to your cosy little spiders' nest? If you see Audmund, take him with you.'

Vargon's face set hard with rage. 'My spiders have had their final dose,' said Vargon, waving his wand in Worfeus' face. 'I'm going to get them now. Seems to me that without them, this will be another garden battle you will lose.'

'I don't need your help, old warlock,' cried Worfeus. 'And remember, when I am king, there won't be any room in my kingdom for you.'

'Your *sister* will be queen, and I'll be by her side as I always was, that is, until you banished her!' said Vargon, squaring up to him. He raised his wand, but

Worfeus beat him to it and cast the Paralysing curse.

The moment it hit him, Vargon knew he was in deep trouble. Looking at Zora, he saw in her cold dark eyes that despite all he had done for her, she had no intention of helping him. She turned and looked away.

Vargon had to find an antidote before the spell took full effect. He shunted directly to his study in Mord Manor, hoping to find something in one of his cupboards. After gulping down a myriad of potions, the ailing warlock shuffled outside. He hurried along as best as he could, as the deadly curse tightened its grip on him. When he reached the courtyard, he took out the whistle he kept in his pocket, and blew on it hard.

Clacking their claws excitedly, Spartax and Spindalux came out of the spiders' nest in the forest. As soon as Vargon saw the two spiders, he realised that Worfeus had given them a double dose of Rage potion. Not even he, their creator, would be able to control them now.

He limped over to the portal just outside the manor wall. Pressing his fingers on a selection of symbols, he blew on the whistle one more time. He threw it into the pulsing portal ring, and just managed to dive out of the way as the spiders followed the shrill sound.

Spartax and Spindalux reappeared in the garden. They smashed their way out of the well, dragging the barbed wire that stuck to their already terrifying armour. The spiders lashed out at the nearest targets, then ran amok through the throngs of fighting warriors.

'At last,' thought Audmund, watching from near the yard. 'Those spiders should cause a stir, though I may need to bring Grizzle here too. I'll need to get closer to that pond if I'm to snatch the orb. Where has Vargon gone now?'

There were duels and fights all over the garden, as the armies realised the temporary freeze on their magic had ended. But any plans of a traditional battle collapsed, as everyone, warlocks and warwitches, wizards and witches, dwarfs and goblins had to run from Spartax and Spindalux. The spiders didn't care who they attacked, they were completely out of control.

A band of dwarfs threw hammers and axes in a coordinated effort, but their weapons didn't make any impact at all.

Zora laughed scornfully. 'Vargon might have enjoyed this,' she said. She looked at her brother. 'Where is he, by the way? What did you do to him?'

'Never mind,' said Worfeus. 'We don't need him, or Audmund for that matter. Let those spiders keep everyone busy. We need to keep an eye on Krag.'

The goblin king hadn't moved from the edge of the pond. The three uneasy allies looked suspiciously at each other. Each of them wanted the orb but they were wary of its power. They needed each other to get it, just in case of trouble, and were secretly afraid of what the orb might unleash.

There was no sign of the orb moving out of the pond. The whining noise grew louder then faded, louder, softer, over and over. Worfeus ordered a few warlocks into the icy water, but they sank in their heavy armour. After they were hauled out, Krag pushed a few goblins in. Their teeth chattered at first with the cold, then they roared and screamed with the burns they got from the glowing orb.

The whining grew shriller after that. All the goblins were moaning with earaches, and the wizards, witches and warlocks frowned as their heads began to throb too. Krag was seething. More goblins were deserting, fed up with waiting for the orb and with having their eardrums pierced a second time.

Worfeus saw trouble mounting for Krag and couldn't resist the chance to rub it in. 'Are you really prepared to risk your throne for a gold lattice?'

'It's our gold,' said Krag. 'I want it back, pure and simple. And I have no intention of losing my throne or my horde.' Stubborn as a mule, the goblin king folded his arms, scowled crossly and continued to stare at the orb.

'I really, really hate spiders,' said Jemima, turning pale. 'Those two look so much quicker and smarter than the last ones we met.'

'Let's hope there are only two,' whispered Abigail.

'They look terrifying but they must have a weakness,' said Luke, firing off a dozen arrows in quick succession at one of the spiders. They flew back to him, having failed to penetrate its armour.

'I agree, but what?' said Jamie. 'I mean where?'

'Even your special arrows are barely sticking to their shell,' said Jemima. 'Nothing is stopping them.'

'I know,' said Luke. 'Only the gold ones stick a bit; the others bounce right off.'

'Spells are useless against them,' said Abigail. 'Vargon

has enhanced those spiders a lot.'

'What about my sword?' asked Jamie.

'Absolutely not,' said Thaddeus, from behind them.

'We have to try,' said Jamie. 'The pets are in real danger. They're no match for monsters and we don't have anything else to stop them.'

'You'd have to get really close,' said Jemima.

'This may be a job for the willow,' said Thaddeus. 'But Wanda has to use it for her duel first, just in case . . .'

'What?' asked Jamie.

Thaddeus hesitated. 'Whoever wins the royal duel can claim the loser's wand.'

'Oh.'

'You mean, Worfeus or Zora could end up with the willow wand?' asked Luke.

'I'm afraid so,' said Thaddeus.

'Where is Aunt Wanda?' asked Abigail, after a short, stunned silence.

'I'm sure she'll be here soon,' said Thaddeus. 'In the meantime, we have to find a way to deal with those spiders.'

'Look!' cried Jamie. 'They're heading for the reindeer, come on.'

He ran down the garden using his shield for protection, dodging all the obstacles, with Luke, Jemima and Abigail close behind him.

'Wait!' cried Thaddeus, but his call was swallowed up in all the noise. He cast a few spells to help unblock their way, but then was caught in a vigorous duel himself.

'If the spiders go after the reindeer,' said Jamie, 'Timber and all the pets will want to help and we won't be able to stop them. We've got to do something now.'

'Look!' cried both the girls. The spiders tossed a few warlocks into the air.

'They don't care who they attack,' said Jamie.

'That's it!' cried Luke. 'It has to be!' He stopped, took aim, then lowered his bow. 'I need to get closer.'

'What has to be?' asked Jamie, running alongside him again, dodging duels, spells and bats.

'Their eyes have to be their weakest point,' said Luke. 'If I can shoot a gold arrow into one eye, then maybe the sword can do the rest.'

'Brilliant!'

It was a daring plan, and Jamie had been right about the pets. All the dogs, cats and foxes were trying to help Sebastian and the herd. It was impossible to call them off in all the noise.

The dogs were getting perilously close as they tried to confuse the spiders so that any reindeer under attack could escape and the other reindeer could try to stab the spiders' underbellies with their antlers. They were all stampeding around the chestnut trees, trying to gain the upper hand. The spiders were exceptionally fast; any four of their eight legs carried them along while the other four legs lashed out in different directions with poisonous talons. They were communicating with each other too, with clacks and spits, planning every move.

As the children neared the herd, Abigail pulled out the crystal key hanging around her neck.

'We definitely need this now,' she said. 'And remember, we have to stay linked together and touching the key to stay protected.'

The key produced its protective shield of light instantly. Slowly and steadily, tucked in tight, the children continued towards the chestnut trees, the charging herd and the two deadly spiders.

'I still can't get a clean shot,' said Luke, changing position again and again, disrupting the shield.

'Hurry up!' cried Jamie. 'The spiders are ferocious! They'll kill all our pets and the reindeer!'

Two reindeer had been too slow to avoid the spiders' talons and were skewered in the neck. They fell, instantly dead. Two others who were scratched were still alive, but it was impossible for Esther to reach them in time in all the chaos.

'No, Timber, no!' cried Jamie, as he watched his dog try to lure one spider away from the herd. Then Jamie realised what Timber was doing. If the spider followed him, Luke would be able to take his shot. He pointed it out to Luke and they watched for the right moment.

The temptation was too much for Spartax. Taking the bait, he broke off from the chase. Spindalux continued clattering after the herd, trying to pick off the slower reindeer first. Sebastian bawled loudly with a mix of rage and fear.

Timber made a daring dash, forcing Spartax to turn and face the children. The spider paused, hissed, clacked four of its talons in the air and charged. Luke leaned out from the shield and fired a gold arrow – a direct hit to one eye. The spider screeched, fell backwards, jerking and twitching as it fell over with a thud. But it wasn't quite dead. Jamie ran over and climbed onto the spider's bulbous head. He raised his sword then slammed it in beside the gold arrow. Spartax squealed, lurched up and fell back down, finally dead. Jamie jumped to safety just before the spider deflated like a huge burst balloon.

Spindalux turned, screeching, eyes bulging. It charged through the trees, smashing and thrashing, but then it skidded to a halt. Spinning around, it turned back towards the chestnut trees, out for revenge.

'Sebastian, look out!' barked Timber.

'No!' cried Teddy. 'Not the stag, NO!'

'We have to bring the pets under this shield,' said Jemima.

'There's no way they'll obey while the reindeer are in trouble,' said Jamie.

'We have to kill the second spider,' said Luke. 'But it won't come near us after what happened the first one. I need to shoot from somewhere else.'

'I'll be right beside you,' said Jamie. He turned to the girls. 'Try to get as many of the pets under this shield as quick as you can.'

Jamie and Luke left the girls and ran to the nearest tree, watching the spider carefully.

The girls called the pets. The foxes and cats made it to the shield easily. The Brigadier and Sylvie were too far away to risk running into the open and getting caught. They hunkered down where they were and waited. Dougal and Trigger reluctantly ran to the shield, and only when Timber barked at them to do so. Timber ignored any calls from Teddy or Jamie to leave the stag.

After a minute or two, Teddy bolted out from the shield, his heart thumping. Timber's promise was on his mind, and the stag was now in mortal danger. He couldn't just watch and do nothing to help.

Jamie stood patiently beside Luke, his sword ready. Luke loaded a gold arrow.

Spindalux caught two more of the herd. With a burst of rage, Sebastian lost control and charged at the spider, Timber at his heels. Teddy ran after them both, skimming around the scattering reindeer. With a loud bawl from the stag, the reindeer reorganised, turned and lowered their heads.

Sebastian tried to lure the spider towards the waiting line of antlers, when suddenly the clever spider spun around and charged at Teddy. His talons had almost caught Teddy's tail, when Gildevard swooped down and snatched the cat out of the way.

Timber realised the spider's new plan, but the stag had already turned and charged at the spider on his own. He roared to the herd to close in once he struck with his antlers.

'Sebastian, no!' barked Timber. 'Wait!'

But the stag didn't hear him. He had to make the spider pay for killing six of the herd. Lowering his head, he aimed for its underbelly, but as he closed in, the spider crouched, leapt over the antlers and caught the stag in the back of his neck with the tip of a talon. Sebastian fell. The children screamed and Timber howled his warning howl.

Sheets of lightning flashed through the grey sky and thunder roared. A favourite of the Ancients had been struck and had fallen. The wind whipped up and crashed through the garden like an instant storm, then it was gone.

The eagle dropped Teddy beside the girls and the pets, and then flew off to the safety of a treetop.

Jemima pulled the cat under the shield. He was mewling loudly. The reindeer tried to reorganise as Spindalux renewed his chase.

'We have to get closer, quickly,' said Luke.

'You saw what happened,' said Jamie. 'That spider is fast and angry.'

'We'll approach under the shield again, then jump out at the last second,' said Luke.

Jamie nodded. 'I'll distract it.'

The children huddled tightly together. Holding on to the animals as well as the key, they struggled to maintain the protective shield. Managing somehow, they moved towards Spindalux.

'Keep the arrow poised,' said Jamie. 'I'll hold you under the shield until you're close enough to fire.'

'OK,' said Luke. 'Just make sure your sword is ready too.'

'You'll only get one chance,' whispered Abigail. 'And I don't think this shield will hold for very long.'

'That beautiful stag,' whispered Jemima, struggling to keep back the tears and keep a hold on a distraught Teddy.

'Poor Sebastian,' said Jamie. 'It's my fault, we should have gone after the spiders before they got near the herd.'

'No,' said Abigail. 'I should have taken out the crystal key sooner.'

'Hush!' said Luke. 'It was no one's fault. Don't move. Here it comes.'

The children and pets stopped in their tracks, perfectly still and silent. Luke took aim as Spindalux moved towards them, clacking its talons menacingly. The spider was only a few feet away, turning its head this way and that, trying to find a weak point in the protective shield. Its eyes bulged, its mouth dribbled, it crouched, preparing to leap.

'NOW!' cried Jamie, and he jumped out from behind the shield. Spindalux was distracted by Jamie's movement, allowing Luke to step out the other side and let the gold arrow fly. It went straight into the spider's right eye.

Jamie rushed forward and slashed at the spiders' legs, hauled himself up its side, then rammed his sword into the eye.

Bushfire and Jugjaw arrived on the scene, their hammers and pickaxes raised. Luke loaded another gold arrow and fired it into the left eye. The spider roared as it half rolled, knocking Jamie off its back. The two dwarfs rushed in as the spider finally collapsed, and they hammered and bashed, making sure it was dead.

The others broke from the shield and ran over to the stag. But there was nothing anyone could do.

'So sad,' whispered Abigail, as she stroked Sebastian's giant antlers.

'What will this mean?' asked Jamie. The animals were howling and whimpering, Oberon screeched mournfully overhead, the other birds were eerily silent.

Their grief was suddenly interrupted by whoops of excitement from Worfeus. The orb wasn't bobbing on the surface any more, it was moving towards the edge of the pond.

Chapter Twenty-two

ROYAL CONTEST

While everyone was either duelling or watching the orb, Wanda and her fairies came up the trap door into the fairy house. They stepped out quietly and surveyed the scene. Their eyes fixed on the orb and the strange beams of coloured light now radiating around the garden. The queen looked a little refreshed, but regardless of how she felt or how the willow might further weaken her, the time had come to face Zora.

'There is no need for more fighting between our clans,' Wanda announced as she walked towards Zora, Worfeus and Krag. 'Everything will be decided by us, the royals.'

Wanda nodded to her fairies. They stepped forward and fired into the air, humming a spell. Every wand flew from its owner and dangled in the air, just out of reach – all except those belonging to Wanda, Zora, Worfeus and Krag.

'Time to show everyone how powerful you are, Zora,' said Worfeus in a loud voice, ensuring everyone would hear. The duel with Wanda would keep his sister occupied while he decided what to do with Krag, once he got the orb.

Zora scowled, then turned to face the Wandelei queen. 'I was beginning to think you were a coward,' she cried.

Wanda raised her wand.

'Ah, the willow,' said Worfeus. 'That explains why you look so awful, Wanda. Even Zora looks younger than you now.'

Zora glared at him, then fired her first spell with a wicked scream. Wanda deftly sidestepped and fired back. The duel was on.

Spells flashed back and forth as each queen battled for the crown, for Grindlewood, and for the orb. Black and red flashes erupted from Zora's wand; Wanda's magic flowed green and turquoise. Both queens were soon scarred by strikes, their gowns sizzling as spells struck. Zora looked the fiercer of the two, Wanda more skilled.

'I will end your reign, once and for all,' cried Zora. 'You, your herbal nut of a sister and that ninny niece of yours – you are all going to die! Take that!'

CRACK! SIZZLE!

Wanda fired back.

FIZZ! CRACKLE! ZIP!

Some warlocks and goblins retreated quietly, their loyalties wavering. No one wanted to be on the losing side, and notions of who would emerge the winner kept changing.

'What are you doing?' Worfeus yelled at his warlocks. 'Finish those Wandeleis!'

But the warlocks ignored him.

Worfeus snorted in disgust. He would deal with them later. He looked at Krag, who was still watching the water. Worfeus didn't trust him, and he knew Krag didn't trust him either. Worfeus hadn't made up his mind how he would deal with the goblin king. It had to be something that wouldn't provoke revenge from the entire goblin horde, and he had to time it carefully too. As for his sister and Wanda, he hoped they would both die in the duel, or at least wear each other out, but very quickly he could see that the two queens were evenly matched. It was impossible to predict the outcome.

Struggling to gain the upper hand, Zora tried to distract Wanda with taunts and insults. Worfeus soon lost patience and started yelling at her.

'No, no, to the left! Duck! No, the other way! Really, Zora, you look like a beginner!'

Zora looked tense. She was furious with her brother, rattled by her opponent, and she had underestimated both the power of the willow and Wanda's skill in controlling it. Then a thought struck her: perhaps she could dispose of both of them at the same time. She shouted to Worfeus.

'Why don't you show me how I should duel, if you're such an expert!'

'Why not?' cried Worfeus, never missing a chance to show off. Zora sneered as he took the bait and jumped into the action. All she had to do now was keep duelling and wait for the right moment.

Fighting two powerful enemies at the same time, Wanda was sorely tested. Her wand was immensely powerful, but already it was tiring her. She wondered how long she could last. And then the duel took an ugly turn.

'This is more of your stupidity!' cried Worfeus, his temper flaring as he too felt the power of the willow. He wondered why his superior magic from Warlock Hell wasn't emerging when he needed it. He wasn't sure what to do next.

'You should have finished this years ago,' cried Zora.

CRACK!

'You let those animals fool you!'

BANG!

'I fooled *you*, didn't I?' Worfeus roared back and fired a triple spell.

SIZZLE, POP, CRACK!

'You never saw it coming. It was my perfect Banishing spell that sent you to the Outer Oblivion. Ha!'

'You despicable rotter!' Zora flicked her wand sideways and fired at Worfeus. 'It's time we sorted out which one of us is really in charge!'

BANG! BANG!

Worfeus howled as he felt his hair momentarily catch fire. He screwed up his face and fired repeatedly at his sister, then at Wanda, then his sister, then Wanda again, over and over, with incredible speed, till the three of them were held in a spell-lock, their wands unable to let go.

Dark purple streams of magic spewed from Worfeus' wand, mixing eerily with the black and red plumes from Zora, and the softer tones from Wanda. The spell-lock ballooned like an umbrella over the three royal duellers. With the coloured rays still beaming from the orb, the garden looked like a weird kaleidoscope.

The bickering continued between brother and sister until eventually Wanda took a chance and broke free.

ZIP! BANG! ZIP! BANG!

She fired with all her might at both opponents, one after the other, but they reacted quicker than she expected. Ignoring each other for a second, they deflected Wanda's spells with lightning speed, bouncing them off around the garden.

Wanda fell to the ground, gasping. Breaking the spell-lock had required a surge of magic, and the willow had nearly sucked her dry of energy.

Pendrick and Thaddeus ran to her, helping her to stand. The fairies clustered together to fend off further incoming spells, but were blasted aside with ease. Both professors were then thrown back with a powerful double blast, one from Worfeus at Pendrick, the other from Zora at Thaddeus. Wanda crumpled to the ground without support. She ordered the fairies to stay away and bravely held up the willow, intending to fight to her last breath.

But Zora and Worfeus stood gloating for too long. Neither could decide whether to kill Wanda or each other first. Their hesitation was enough for Wanda to be spared a Killing spell, and then cries and shrieks erupted from beside the pond. They were followed by a triumphant roar from Krag, which drew everyone's attention.

The orb had rolled out of the water and the whining noise stopped. Everything stopped. Even the royal wands and the fairy wands fell to the ground, disabled.

The Wandeleis gathered slowly at one end of the pond, any remaining Worfagons at the other. In the middle on the edge of the scorched grass was Othelia's Orb.

'Ouch!' said Jamie.

'What's wrong?' asked Luke.

Jamie pointed to his chest. 'My key is so hot, it burned me.'

‘It’s being called to do something,’ said Abigail.

‘To burn me?’ said Jamie.

‘No, no,’ said Abigail. ‘Something else, something important. I wonder . . .’

Jamie was watching Abigail, wondering what she meant, when Timber pawed at his knee.

‘Maybe he knows,’ said Jemima.

Timber barked at the dwarfs, then turned to Teddy and the dogs. ‘Worfeus mentioned the key earlier,’ said Timber. ‘We mustn’t let the Worfagons or the goblins take it.’

‘We’ll do whatever you say, Timber,’ said Bushfire, bustling over, his face red from all his efforts.

Jugjaw nodded beside him. ‘There’s no telling what kind of magic is in that orb,’ he said, ‘but the queen said we’re to do what you tell us. We all will.’

Worfeus stomped over to them, wild-eyed, furious. The dwarfs scowled at him, their big hands curled into fists. Timber growled angrily and Worfeus stopped.

‘I want that key!’ Worfeus cried. ‘We were interrupted earlier when I asked for it politely, and I won’t ask nicely again. Come on, hand it over.’ He scanned each of the Grindlewood Army, his red eyes boring into them.

Krag knew what the gold key was needed for; the goblins had made it too. His eyes searched the crowd, trying to spot the holder of the key, or the key itself.

Zora stomped around, swishing her skirts and looking like thunder. 'Ignore them,' she said. 'I will give a reward for the key. Well? Tell me who has it. Who?' She picked up her wand, then threw it on the ground again. 'How is that orb controlling our wands? What happened to your hell-born magic, Worfeus? We could use some of it now.'

'I don't know,' roared Worfeus. 'The orb has its own magic, and I want it, I WANT IT NOW!'

'It's even controlling your wand, Krag,' said Claw, glaring into his face. He turned and sneered at the dwarfs next. They were struggling to raise their hammers off the ground, but their weapons didn't respond either. The orb had brought all fighting to a halt.

Timber growled another warning growl and looked at Jamie. Before Jamie could even think of what to do, Worfeus made his move.

'*I* don't always need to use a wand, Retrus Aurum!' Worfeus cried and he waved his hand in a wide arc, then pulled it to his chest in a tight fist.

Jamie felt the gold key vibrate under his sweater. Slowly, he raised a hand to his chest to calm it, hoping his movement wouldn't be noticed.

Zora was certain that the key would come to her. 'Retrus Aurum!' she cried.

Jamie felt another lunge, but without a wand, the spell wasn't strong enough to pull the key away.

'Retrievo Aurum!' cried Wanda, using the Wandelei spell, as she staggered to her feet. The key did not fly to her either. It spun on the string around Jamie's neck, tightening till he had to stop it from choking him.

'There!' cried Zora. 'The boy beside Jemumble!'

'Her name is Jemima,' roared Jamie, after he loosened the string.

Timber stood in front of Jamie, his growls growing to angry barks. Dougal, Trigger and Teddy closed in beside him, forming a barrier in front of the four children. Timber turned and stood on his hind paws to take the key from Jamie, but Krag had been waiting more patiently than the rest. He darted forward and called the key in goblin tongue. To cries of horror, the key flew up Jamie's neck, broke from the string and hovered in mid-air beside all the floating wands. It had been made by a goblin and recognised a goblin's call

– a little trick the goblins kept secret whenever they made anything.

Immediately there was a furious scramble. Worfeus, Zora, Wanda, the professors, and a few goblins, including Krag, all tried to call the key. When that failed, they all tried to reach for it. Even the children and dwarfs tried to jump and grab it, but the little gold key twitched in the air out of everyone's reach, as if trying to make up its mind who to choose.

Timber barked to Dougal and Trigger. The two dogs stood side by side, and Timber jumped up on their backs and leapt as high as he could, snatching the key out of the air. He spat it out at Jamie's feet, but before Jamie could pick it up, Krag called the key again and it flew to him along the ground.

The goblin king grabbed the key and made a dash for the orb. Worfeus dived clumsily to stop him, afraid that whoever opened the lattice would claim the power of the orb.

Zora had the same idea. She pushed Wanda aside, desperate to stop anyone reaching the orb before she did. Worfeus and Zora both grappled with Krag, rolling around on the ground, tearing at each other, wanting to be the one who placed the gold key into the gold lattice.

Worfeus managed to trip Krag, who fell and dropped the key, making the scramble even more furious. Pendrick helped Wanda up and they too joined in, but they couldn't even get close as Zora, Worfeus and Krag and a few goblins tossed and kicked it about in a panic.

Zora's flouncy gown was getting in everyone's way. Krag scurried around all the kicking feet and grappling hands, and crawled after the orb on his hands and knees under the pile of scramblers. With a roll and a lunge at full stretch, he grabbed the key and placed it into the lattice.

The elaborate gold lace immediately uncoiled like a long snake. The gold key fell away and Trigger, quick as a dart, ran forward and snatched it up.

'Give it to the queen,' barked Timber. Trigger obeyed, but was it too late? Had the goblin king won the prize?

Bolts of lightning shot from the orb, keeping greedy hands away. Unable to grasp it, Worfeus and Zora went for the lattice and tried to rip it free from Krag's hands. They screamed and roared at each other, pulling and tugging, till eventually the lattice broke free of them all. It took to the sky, flying around like a kite.

Everyone had a bad feeling when it halted overhead. It hovered for a moment, then hurtled back towards the earth with intent. It had a target.

The crowd broke apart and even Zora and Worfeus scurried for cover. The lattice straightened out like a long harpoon and hurtled after Krag. The key might have answered Krag's call, but the lattice had been enchanted to protect the orb at all costs.

The lattice quickly gained on the goblin king, who barely had time to turn and run. It caught him easily, twisting around, binding him like a rope, and pulled him into the air. Krag wriggled and fought but to no avail. The lattice tightened around his body, strangling him in its grip, then dropped him to the ground – dead. The goblin king burned in a sudden flash, then disappeared.

Whipping through the air in a murderous rage, the lattice hovered again, looking for more targets. Stretched wide like a giant net, it caught five goblins just before they popped and escaped. It bound them tight and crushed them like Krag.

The lattice twirled in the sky before plummeting to earth again. Any remaining goblins who hadn't already fled assumed they were next. With lightning speed, it picked off dozens. Then it started on the warlocks, strangling them like a snake in mid-air or smothering them in its widespread net.

'Stay out of its path, you idiots!' roared Worfeus, but few of his army were listening any more.

'This is your fault!' cried Zora. 'Everything is your fault! You brought the goblins in on this, you and Audmund, and that lattice doesn't like them!'

'This would not have happened if I had opened the lattice,' Worfeus roared. 'Your ridiculous gown got in my way, and that greedy goblin got to it first!' He glared at his sister and wanted to kill her there and then, but the orb was still blocking their magic.

Wanda turned to her professors. 'Gentlemen, we must get the orb.'

'We can't know what that lattice may do, Your Majesty,' said Pendrick.

'Though Krag called the key and placed it on the lattice, it still chose to kill him,' said Sparks.

'It might kill all of us,' said a flustered Flint.

'Do you think things will improve if the Worfagons

get it?' asked Wanda impatiently. 'We must find a way.'

'I believe we can,' said Thaddeus.

The others looked at him, hoping he had the answer.

'The goblins and the warlocks tried to take the orb out of the pond, but we didn't,' he explained. 'That's why the lattice attacked them but not us. Now, the orb is in control.'

'I think you could be right,' said the queen. 'That changes things.'

'You mean the lattice won't attack us?' said Flint.

'And we just have to worry about the orb, right?' said Sparks.

'But we don't really know what the orb wants, do we?' said Pendrick.

'The orb blocked our wands, but that enchantment cannot last much longer,' said Wanda. 'We must be ready for anything once the enchantment ends.'

'Perhaps Timber and the children can help,' said Thaddeus, 'but it's a risk.'

'My thoughts exactly,' said Wanda. 'Go to them, Thaddeus.'

The lightning had stopped spiking from the orb, but it was on the move again, rolling slowly and silently along the edge of the pond towards the end of the garden. It stopped near the granite stone. The last rays of colourful light went out. Everyone reached for their wands and weapons, hoping their magic might be restored. It was.

'If they get the orb, we are done for,' said Zora, in a rasping whisper.

'*We*?' said Worfeus. 'You said you would deal with Wanda. Get on with it! I'll get the orb.'

'Don't even think of taking it without me,' said Zora, 'or I will kill you.'

'Likewise,' said Worfeus.

Zora turned, whipped her wand through the air and fired. But Wanda was ready for a fast strike and blocked it. Immediately the queens resumed their duel in earnest, but no one else did. After seeing what the lattice could do, everyone wanted to run or hide and let the two queens fight it out.

Worfeus ignored them and watched the orb.

Thaddeus found the children, but they had already decided what must be done.

'Granddad,' said Abigail, 'we have to get close to the orb.'

'It came out from under the reeds when we spoke

to it before,' said Jemima. 'We think we should talk to it again.'

Thaddeus didn't argue. 'Go now,' he said. 'Follow Timber's lead. He will know what to do, but please be careful.'

Chapter Twenty-three

TIMBER'S CHOICE

With Krag gone, the horde cared little about what happened to the orb or the lattice. All except a few wounded goblins had already left or been killed by the lattice. The dwarfs took the rest as prisoners and hauled them off to the new dungeon in Hollow Hill.

It was a similar fate for several warlocks and warwitches. A few had been killed by the lattice; others had abandoned the fight and fled; the remainder were either exhausted or injured and surrendered willingly.

But the real question on everyone's mind was, what would happen with the orb? If it were as powerful as feared, it could affect everyone, the future of Grindlewood.

Without his army's support, Worfeus grew anxious

as well as impatient. He decided to join Wanda and Zora's duel to hurry things along. 'I'll finish these two,' he thought. 'No one will dare stop me taking the orb when I'm the winner.' He strode towards Wanda and Zora and fired his way into the duel.

Wanda, Zora and Worfeus cast a sizzling array of spells. It was a furious, angry triple-fight, dangerous even to watch. With so many spells firing so rapidly, the three wands became locked again. Everyone watching was held in suspense, waiting to see who was truly the most powerful.

The willow's superiority finally won out and Wanda broke the hold. She ducked, rolled and fired a Split spell, but miscalculated, and was exposed for just one second. Thaddeus and Pendrick jumped in to defend her. Timber also leapt across to protect her, managing to knock Wanda out of direct firing line. Pendrick was hit on the shoulder. Thaddeus groaned as he was struck in the back.

On her knees, Wanda held the willow in both hands and fired. 'Destorastum Willositum!' she cried, falling over with the sheer force of the willow's Killing spell.

Worfeus and Zora were stunned. Having stood side by side, they were thrown apart and off their feet by the blast, their faces still set with surprise. There was a strange stillness in Grindlewood as the twins hung in the air, before disintegrating into nothing. They were gone. Dead.

Pendrick wasn't badly hurt, but Wanda had been almost knocked unconscious by the force of the spell. Sparks and Flint helped them both to their feet. Timber stood over Thaddeus, howling for attention. The professor had taken much of the force of Zora's Killing spell. Abigail let out a cry and ran to her granddad.

Wanda raised the willow and tried to chant a Healing spell for Thaddeus, but she was still too weak. Esther and Tamara applied their tinctures, but nothing seemed to work.

'There must be something else we can do,' cried Abigail.

'The diamond!' cried Luke.

'Yes!' cried Jemima, and she pulled it out of her pocket.

'Just as well we didn't waste it after all,' said Jamie. He clapped Luke on the shoulder. 'You were right.'

Jemima held out the gemstone. Tears were streaming down Abigail's face.

'You do it, Jamie,' said Abigail. 'I can't, I can't.'

Jamie took the gemstone. 'I'll get it right,' he said. 'I promise.' Clenching his fist tightly, he closed his eyes and wished for the professor to be healed. Everyone waited, hoping. There was no guarantee it would undo Zora's Killing spell.

After what seemed like an age, Thaddeus muttered a little, but he didn't wake up. He didn't look well at all.

'I was so sure it would work,' said Luke.

'So was I,' said Jamie. 'I'm sorry, Abi, I'm so sorry.'

'Don't say sorry,' said Jemima. 'He's just sleeping, you'll see. He'll be OK. We have to believe.' She looked hopefully at the others, but no one could find any words. They didn't find it as easy to believe as she always did.

'Children,' said Wanda gently. 'Let the gemstone work its magic, but be patient. I must perform an enchantment on the stag. It is tradition when a magical creature of such importance has fallen. I will return in a moment. Esther and Tamara will stay with you.' The queen motioned to Pendrick, Flint and Sparks. They helped her over to where the stag lay amongst the chestnut trees, the herd gathered silently around him.

Teddy meowed loudly at Timber. 'The gemstone could have saved Sebastian,' he said. 'Then you wouldn't have to leave us, Timber. Please say you won't go.'

The pets stared at Timber, wondering what Teddy meant. When he explained about his promise, they were devastated.

'Why make a promise?' said Dougal. 'Wouldn't they help us anyway?'

'The stag is part of the ancient magical world,' said Timber. 'They have rules that must be obeyed.'

'But what good will that do him now?' barked Eldric. 'And we need you here.'

'Can't they choose a new leader from the herd?' asked the Brigadier.

'I made a promise to Sebastian, and I must keep it,' said Timber.

'Can't you get out of it somehow?' cried Teddy.

'Breaking a vow with a magical creature would bring terrible consequences,' said Oberon. 'I don't see how it can be undone.'

'That orb has brought us nothing but trouble,' cried Norville.

Timber looked over at the orb. He felt it pulling him, calling him. He turned to the pets. 'I think

I understand the orb and what it can do. Do not approach, no matter what happens. Understood?'

'Um, no?' said Dougal.

'What are you going to do?' asked Teddy.

'Trust me, please, like you always have,' said Timber.

'Hey, where's Timber going?' cried Jamie. 'Timber!'

Timber ran towards the orb. Teddy went gingerly after him, not wanting to disobey but not wanting Timber to be alone whatever he was up to. The animals fell quiet. The birds flew down from the trees to join them. Together they waited nervously.

'Something weird is going on,' said Jamie. 'Why is Timber ignoring me?'

Esther explained Timber's promise as gently as she could.

'What? No! NO! Timber can't leave!' cried Jamie. 'He can't! I won't let him!'

'Don't take Timber away, please,' said Jemima.

'It was Timber's promise, Timber's choice,' said Esther. 'No one made him do it. He wanted to ensure the garden would be safe, and all of you too.'

'It wasn't his fault the stag was killed,' said Luke.

'But that isn't fair,' cried Jemima. 'He can't. Oh no.'

Jamie ran after Timber but stopped short before

reaching him. If Timber had a plan, an interruption might endanger his dog. Another thing stopped Jamie. The butterflies had landed on the orb. 'What could they possibly have to say now?' he thought.

The orb sat at the edge of the pond, waiting for Timber. There was no whining any more, no lightning, no light. Just the butterflies, perched calmly on top. Timber sniffed it, pawed it; the orb did not react. Then the butterflies rose and landed on Timber's head. They spoke to him, though their voices sounded different this time, and no one else could hear them.

'Timber, Guardian of Grindlewood, I am trapped inside this orb and you are the only one who can free me. This journey was written in the Ancients' prophecy, but the end is up to you. And the end is now.'

Timber noticed ribbons of colour moving slowly around inside the orb, the colours of the rainbow, just like the butterflies.

'To free me, you must destroy me,' it said, again through the butterflies. 'You must find a way, so it is written. In return you will receive my knowledge, my power – and immortality. This is also written.'

Timber was shocked. The fate of the orb was

entirely in his hands, and it was all in the prophecy. He thought how Queen Wanda had been so desperate to find it, and he rememebered her words: 'You will know what to do when the time comes.' She had been trying to tell him about the prophecy. Zora and Worfeus had wanted the orb too; so had Krag, Vargon and Audmund. It had caused so much trouble and death. Did anyone deserve it?

The orb spoke through the butterflies again. 'To free me, you must destroy me. To free me, you must destroy me.' Timber heard the phrase repeated over and over again, 'Free me, destroy me. Free me, destroy me . . .' in a pleading voice that wouldn't stop.

Timber looked at Wanda's anxious face. He really wanted to help her and her clan. But in his heart he knew that if anyone had the orb, there would be more battles in the future, dreadful battles that might never end. But if he destroyed the orb, he would be given all these gifts, gifts like immortality, and he would outlive everyone he knew and loved, watch them die and be alone. He didn't want that, he didn't want any of it.

'Free me, destroy me, free me . . .'

Teddy ran over to Timber, unable to stay away any longer. The dogs and cats followed, all of them unsure what Timber was about to do.

But the bravest dog in the world had made up his mind. He looked at the granite stone a short distance away. It had a special place in Grindlewood garden. 'Yes, I know what to do,' he thought. Lowering his shoulders, he leaned into the orb and pushed it along the ground. It began to roll, but only because Timber was pushing it; the orb could not decide its own fate.

Above the garden, the golden eagle was circling, screeching. 'NO! Timber, NO!' cried Gildevard.

Timber ignored him. The eagle was in such a panic, he forgot about the lattice which was hovering directly over the orb. As he flew down, the lattice plucked him from the sky, and held him in a tight grip. The orb sent a bolt of lightning up to the lattice, dissolving it into tiny particles of gold that fell onto the granite stone. The orb didn't need protection any more. There would be no more killing.

Gildevard flew quickly into a tree, more shaken than he had ever been.

'Why did the orb do that?' barked Trigger.

'It doesn't need the lattice any more,' said Eldric.

'Um, what's the orb going to do now?' asked Dougal.

'And what is Timber going to do?' asked Ramona. Dozens of rabbits had followed her out of their hiding places. The garden was full of animals and birds again, all of them closing in on the orb and Timber.

'Oh, dear!' said Oberon. 'I think I've just figured it out, but I wish I hadn't. We can't be sure what will happen when the magic is released.'

'Released?' said Eldric.

'Oh, Timber,' thought Teddy. 'Don't be so brave, just this once.'

Luke left Esther and the girls and joined Jamie. Jemima followed but Abigail stayed beside her granddad, holding his hand. He still hadn't woken up.

Timber barked his danger bark and pawed at the ground. Like the snowy owl, he wasn't sure what would happen once the magic, or whatever was inside the orb, was set free.

He turned and gave the orb another shove with his paw this time, then another, speeding it up, rolling faster and faster along the edge of the pond. Timber turned suddenly and kicked the orb hard with his back legs, driving it into the granite stone. It smashed with a 'BOOM!' and a burst of coloured light.

Everyone gasped. Othelia's Orb was destroyed.

Chapter Twenty-four

RAINBOW MAGIC

Once the orb was broken, the rainbow inside was set free. Escaping from its centuries-old prison, it stretched long and wide, proudly displaying its seven colours in all their splendour.

The rainbow gathered up like a huge wave, then hurled itself back towards the ground. There were frightened screams as everyone remembered what the lattice had done. But the rainbow only swirled around the garden, overjoyed to be free again. It slowed to a halt in front of Timber, and spoke to him through the butterflies, when they landed again on his head. 'You have freed me, Timber, Guardian of Grindlewood. In return I must endow you with my power, knowledge and immortality.'

'No, wait,' barked Timber. The rainbow halted just above him. 'If I may, I would wish for something else.'

'Who would wish for anything more?' asked the rainbow.

'Not more, and not for me,' said Timber. 'For my friends.'

Timber knew exactly what he wanted: Thaddeus well again and the stag returned from the jaws of death, but he wasn't sure he could have both.

'You must choose,' said the rainbow, sensing his unease.

Timber looked around at all his friends, the Grindlewood Army. He saw Teddy's sad, pleading face and the dogs whimpering beside him. Jamie looked very upset, his heart breaking at the thought of losing his beautiful dog. Luke and Jemima stood beside him. Jemima was on the verge of tears and Luke had turned very pale. Abigail was sobbing in her mother's arms, thinking her granddad would surely die. The reindeer stood quietly around Sebastian, waiting for the queen to enchant him.

Timber felt frozen in time as he saw everyone,

waiting, watching him, and then Wanda's words came back to him again. 'You will know what to do, Timber. Only the journey is written by the Ancients; the end will be up to you.' The rainbow had said something similar and now it was time to choose.

Timber's thoughts were disturbed when Thaddeus give a little cough and a splutter. He watched Esther and Tamara help the professor sit up and hand him another potion. Both of the witches were smiling, so was Abigail.

Timber looked up at the rainbow. 'Thank you for offering me such generous gifts,' he said, 'but I believe they should remain with you. My only wish is for the stag to be returned to us, just as he was before.'

'It is a noble wish,' said the rainbow, 'and I shall grant it.'

Timber bounded over to the fallen stag. The rainbow followed, curving and swirling through the trees till it reached the spot. Timber barked to the herd and explained what was agreed.

The reindeer formed a wide circle. As the rainbow billowed over the wounded Sebastian, Timber howled to call the pets to join them. The animals hurried forward, tucking in beside the herd, Teddy beside

Timber. The birds perched in the branches of the surrounding chestnut trees. Jamie stood beside Timber, his hand resting on his collar. Luke and Jemima stood close by. Glancing back at Abigail, they saw that she was laughing now and drying her face.

'Go,' said Thaddeus, as Esther handed him another potion and Tamara waved her wand over his head. At last, a rosy blush was returning to the professor's cheeks. 'Quickly, dear. This is a special moment in magical history.'

Abigail gave her granddad a hug and ran to her friends.

'A rainbow!' said Thaddeus, looking at Esther and Tamara. 'Who'd have thought it? Please, help me up, ladies, I don't want to miss this moment either.'

Timber woofed softly and moved a little closer, as the rainbow poised over the stag.

'Timber is talking to a rainbow,' whispered Jemima, her face lit up with wonder.

Abigail appeared beside her and squeezed her hand.

'Unbelievable,' whispered Luke.

Jamie looked adoringly at his dog. He felt so proud of him, but anxious too, unsure if Timber was still going to leave. Timber turned and looked at him.

It was his gentle look, telling Jamie to trust him, all would be well. Jamie took a deep breath and Luke gave his friend a little puck on the shoulder.

'It'll be OK,' whispered Luke.

'I hope so,' said Jamie.

The rainbow sank down and wrapped itself around Timber and the stag until they were hidden from view. A warm breeze ruffled through the chestnut trees and caressed the watching group. The rainbow worked its magic and granted Timber's wish.

When the breeze departed, the rainbow unfurled and drifted up to the sky. The clouds split apart, some melted away, and a few spilled their raindrops. Then the sun peeped out. The rainbow formed a huge, wide arc over the garden.

Timber howled his happy howl and the dogs joined in. Sebastian bawled hoarsely as he tried to stand up. A few reindeer nudged him to his hooves, then they all clustered around him. No one was happier than Teddy. He nearly choked on his meows and purrs as he snuggled into Timber.

'I never expected a rainbow,' said Wanda.

'No mention of it in the puzzle either,' said Pendrick.

‘We are privileged,’ said Flint. ‘This may never be seen again.’

‘I knew Timber would make the right choice, whatever happened,’ said Wanda. ‘No one should have the rainbow’s magic, not now, not ever.’

‘I can’t imagine how Othelia did it,’ said Sparks. ‘Trapping the rainbow in an orb like that.’

‘Both Oscar and Othelia were extraordinary,’ said Pendrick. ‘But their genius did cause a lot of trouble.’

‘And death and destruction,’ said Thaddeus, joining them, Esther and Tamara at his side. ‘Rainbows belong to the universe and should always be free.’

Sebastian bowed low to Timber and rubbed his antlers against the dog’s happy face. ‘Thank you, Timber,’ he said. ‘I owe you my life.’

‘You risked your life and your herd for us,’ said Timber. ‘We will always be indebted to you.’

The stag nodded. ‘We must depart for the Eastern Woods once it is dark. Until then, we will rest a while and enjoy some of those chestnuts!’ He looked around to where several reindeer were already munching.

Timber turned to the children and was smothered in hugs. Jemima tried to cuddle Teddy too, but he was too excited to stay still.

Suddenly, Peabody ran out to the garden all in a dither. He hadn't been able to stop Greg and Gloria barging past him, demanding to know what was going on in their own house. He hurried outside to warn everyone, but the Grindles were right behind him.

'Oh, my word,' said Greg. 'Our lovely garden!' He looked around and then up. 'Isn't that rainbow rather close?'

'It sure was,' muttered Jamie, stifling a laugh.

'How do we explain this?' whispered Luke.

'Granddad will fix it,' said Abigail.

'Why don't we just tell them?' said Jemima.

The others looked at her.

'Do we have to keep everything a secret forever?' asked Jemima.

'Probably,' said Jamie. 'Mum and Dad would never understand.'

'Not like we do,' said Luke, with a grin.

'Jamie, Jemima, introduce us to all your new friends,' said Gloria, smiling at everyone.

'Er, sure,' said Jamie.

Jemima was about to begin a very long list of names as the fairies crept up behind Greg and Gloria, and cast a Memory-wipe spell.

Thaddeus smiled broadly, flashing his gold tooth. It was working again, better than ever. 'Perhaps we should go inside and have some of Esther's hot chocolate,' he said.

'Wonderful idea,' said Gloria. 'Come along, everyone!'

Behind her, the fairies smiled at each other. They were delighted with their new gentle, but effective, spell. There would be no more worries about too much memory mist.

'Excellent!' said Greg. 'Good to see you again, Peabody!'

Thaddeus and Peabody went inside with Greg and Gloria, while the fairies, Flint and Sparks cast several spells around the garden to tidy it up. Esther and Tamara assisted the last of the wounded, then went inside too. The children, Timber and Teddy ran in after them, happy to see the garden returning to normal.

Pendrick sent everyone else back to Hollow Hill and then walked over to the well. It was a sorry sight.

‘We can’t leave you looking like this,’ he whispered. ‘Not when you were once a prime portal.’ He cast a Fix-it spell, and the well was good as new. He spotted a tiny glint at the bottom of the well shaft. With a flick of his new mahogany wand, he called it to the surface. It was Vargon’s old whistle. ‘Aha,’ he said. ‘Sparks and I will have fun examining this.’

Chapter Twenty-five

IN THE END

Audmund never returned to Grindlewood. The second dose of Rage potion made Grizzle completely uncontrollable and he attacked his own master, goring him with his poisonous tusks. Audmund was killed instantly, then the dwarf-troll keeled over too – death by potion poisoning.

When Vargon returned to the manor seeking an antidote for the Paralysing curse, one of his other spiders surprised him in the courtyard. Pouncing like a hunting animal, it stabbed him with an extra-long talon.

'I wonder what will kill me first?' thought the old lord. 'Worfeus' spell, or one of my own creations? Ha! Haa-agh, aaaghhh!'

Unable to walk any longer, Vargon used his onyx ring to transport himself inside. But despite all the clever concoctions in his cupboard, it was too late to find a cure. Cursing himself for having bothered to bring Zora back at all, Vargon died in his favourite armchair, with Bodric looking on, bemused.

The buzzard knew the game was up. Careful to avoid the marauding spider, he leapt through the portal in the nick of time. Without Vargon's magic to sustain it, the private dimension collapsed and disappeared. Bodric would need to lie low for a while, but as always, he would find a way to survive.

Ripley was snatched by one of the goblins who managed to escape the garden. The squirrel was poor compensation for lost gold, but he was taken nonetheless. His future did not look bright.

Gildevard flew to his cliff-top nest, without saying goodbye. No one knew whose side he had been on; it was possible the eagle didn't even know himself.

With all the excitement over Christmas, it was

another few days before the queen had a chance to thank the Grindlewood Army properly. While their parents were snoozing by the fire (after a relaxing herbal tea), the children, dogs, cats, foxes, Oberon and Ramona hurried down the trap door and along the tunnels to Hollow Hill.

A sumptuous supper awaited them. Afterwards Queen Wanda made a lovely speech, thanking the children for their loyalty, bravery and friendship, and she promised more peaceful times ahead. 'Brilliant though Oscar and Othelia were,' the queen continued, 'they were wrong to trap a rainbow, one of the most magical creations in the universe. But thanks to all of you, and especially our brave guardian, Timber, the rainbow is free, the orb and its secrets are part of history, and our enemies are gone. Grindlewood is safe again.'

Before they left, the children returned the four keys.

'They did have more magic,' said Luke, handing over the iron key.

'And we really needed it,' said Jamie. He felt a little sad giving up the gold key; he had got used to it hanging around his neck.

'The keys' magic will only help the *worthy,*' said Wanda. 'You are so important to us – you, all your pets, and especially Timber.' Timber trotted over to the queen and licked her hands. She smiled at him. 'Never forget how special you are, and always keep each other safe.'

Wanda placed the keys back in their wooden box, and locked it away in her private vault.

Next morning, on New Year's Eve, Thaddeus arrived at the Grindles' house with a gift.

'Lovely piece of work,' said Greg, admiring the carpentry.

'Thank you,' said Thaddeus. 'It's the third one I've made. I thought the children could put all their special things in it. The fairy house is getting very full, I hear.' Thaddeus winked at the children.

They knew what the box was at once – an Invisibility chest.

'Thanks, Mr Allnutt,' said Jamie. 'We'll put George's things in there, with, the, eh, other stuff.' He meant all their magical things, the sword, shield, bow, arrows, wands, and all the other magical gifts.

'Will there be enough room for everything?' asked Greg.

'This chest holds more than you'd think,' said Thaddeus, grinning again.

'Terrific!' said Greg. 'Everything in its proper place at last. We're finally getting everything sorted.'

'I'll bring it through to the fairy house, if you don't mind putting on the kettle,' said Thaddeus.

Greg went back to the house to organise the tea. Thaddeus had a quick word with the children as they walked with him to the fairy house.

'We'll take good care of it, Professor,' said Jemima.

'It takes care of itself, my dear,' said Thaddeus. 'As you already know, everything you put inside will be invisible, so best not to let your parents look in without having an excuse ready. It would be a good place to hide the gold, by the way, at least until we figure out how to explain it.'

'Good idea,' said Jamie, looking over at the crate in the corner. 'Let's do that now.'

The boys unloaded the crate of gold and placed each piece carefully into the Invisibility chest.

'I'm glad Professor Flint took away the bones,' said Jemima.

'Yes,' said Thaddeus, raising his eyebrows. 'He likes to study unusual things and those bones should keep him busy.'

All through the holidays, the children spoke about their latest quest. They wondered about the rainbow too.

'We should have guessed that rainbows were magical,' said Jemima.

'When do you think we'll be called to help again?' asked Luke.

'Not too soon, according to the queen,' said Jamie.

'How many secrets are still out there?' asked Jemima, glancing at the window.

'Lots,' said Abigail.

The boys looked curiously at the two girls.

'It's possible,' said Jemima.

'It's not something I know for sure,' said Abigail. 'But I wouldn't be surprised.'

'I agree,' said Luke. 'We can't have discovered everything. Even the giant puzzle isn't finished.'

'I wonder if Timber knows more than we do,' said Jamie. 'He's always been the most important one in all of this.' Timber stood up and put his front paws on Jamie's lap. 'Yep, I'm sure he does, but he'll tell us when the time's right. Won't you?'

'Yes,' barked Timber, and he gave Jamie a generous lick.

Jemima reached for the big history book. It had been updating a lot recently. There were several mentions of their latest quest and there was even a picture of Timber. 'Our story will turn into witch language soon,' she said. 'Will I read it one more time while we still can?'

The other dogs came in to the fairy house and sat on the floor, the cats on laps, and the foxes and hedgehog huddled in the corner. The rabbits covered the entire porch and whatever space they could find inside. The birds perched on the bookshelves and windowsills. The fairy house was full to the brim, everyone happy to hear about another successful adventure.

Outside, the three Grindlewood butterflies flew down the garden for the last time. They snuggled into the hedge beside the bee hive. Their work was done and this would be their final sleep.

Pendrick accompanied Wanda to the goblins' labyrinth of tunnels. The queen used the willow to destroy every trace of them, including the criminal court. After so much embarrassment, it was unlikely the goblins would return. She checked the rest of the tunnels, ensuring they were closed, save only for two – one to the fairy house and one to the Allnutts' cellar.

Alone in her private chamber that night, Wanda opened her *Book of Prophecies*. So many had come true, but luckily the one about Timber leaving the garden had not. 'The future is not as set as the prophecies might suggest,' she thought. 'I have learned an important lesson.'

She turned the pages slowly. Some had turned blank as one wrong from the past was made right again. There were pictures of the children, each on a separate page, their futures already mapped out. Or were they? Grindlewood would be quiet for a while, but that was a good thing. The children needed to live normal lives too, at home with their parents and with their pets, but they would always be the *worthy*.

Timber stood in the middle of the garden and howled a happy howl to the night. He trotted back to the kennel, his paws crunching softly on the frosty grass.

Dougal was dreaming, murmuring, his ears twitching. The Brigadier was snoring softly like he always did. Teddy was still awake, waiting for him. He hadn't slept in the house for a while now; he had been so worried about losing his best friend.

'Do you think we can just be pets for a while?' he asked.

'We will always be the Grindles' pets,' said Timber. 'And we will always be the Guardians of Grindlewood too. That is our destiny.'

Teddy snuggled in beside him, purring contentedly, till they both fell asleep. Outside all was quiet and still, as the first snow of the new year began to fall.

THE END

Acknowledgements

A huge thank you to all the team: Robert Doran (editor), Chenile Keogh (Kazoo), Vanessa O'Loughlin (Inkwell), Fintan Taite (illustrator), Andrew Brown and Nigel Baker (graphic design).

Thank you to all the bookstores, schools and libraries that continue to support my work, and all the enthusiastic young readers who enjoy the story of Grindlewood.

A special mention for my friend, Peri Burnside, who introduced me to the real Timber, and also for my husband Angelo, my biggest fan, supporter, advisor and best friend.

Book 1

THE SECRETS OF GRINDLEWOOD

Jamie and Jemima Grindle move to Grindlewood House with their pets Timber and Teddy. But they soon realise that all is not as it seems in their beautiful new garden. There is dark magic at work in the nearby forest.

The good witch Wanda has been defeated and now the wicked warlock Worfeus is plotting to destroy Grindlewood and its enchanted garden. Only Wanda's powerful spells, written on a secret scroll, can rid the world of the warlock.

Timber must lead the animals of Grindlewood in their quest to find the scroll and defeat their enemy. But where is the scroll hidden and will they find it before Worfeus? Is there really enough magic in their wild garden to help them defeat such evil?

THE SECRET SCROLL

Grindlewood Book 2: The Secret Scroll follows the animals of Grindlewood garden as they continue the quest to save their enchanted home. The odds are stacked against them as they struggle to understand the ancient language of Wanda's secret scroll and use its magic to defeat the evil Worfeus.

Slowly Jamie and Jemima learn that their pets are caught up in something both sinister and special and that somehow they must find a way to help. All the while, the wicked warlock is growing more powerful and threatening.

The race is on to unlock the secrets of the scroll before Worfeus frees himself from the forest and enters the garden himself, intent on revenge and the destruction of Grindlewood.

Book 3

THE QUEEN'S QUEST

When she hears that the residents of Grindlewood garden have defeated the wicked warlock Worfeus, the Forest Queen decides to enlist their help to release her from the Worfagons' curse. But it soon becomes clear that the Queen is not the kind and gentle leader she once was.

After years of suffering under the Worfagon 'tree spell', the Queen is now bitter and angry. She is obsessed with Jamie's beautiful dog, Timber, and she threatens to keep him for herself unless the children agree to come to her aid. They must find the lost *Ancient Book of Magic*, which holds powerful spells that can free her.

Timber the brave malamute dog once again leads Jamie, Jemima and their loyal band of pets in a hair-raising adventure. Together they must face down mortal danger, dark magic and evil enemies to free the trapped Forest Queen and ensure Timber's safe return.

Book 4

Zora's Revenge

While the sorceress Zora plans her revenge, the peace-loving Wandeleis find their magic is dangerously unstable. Unsure if they can match Zora's growing powers, they must prepare for a frightening encounter.

With another traitor in their midst and more of their treasures missing, it isn't long before the Wandeleis' magic is tested. They know their enemies are closing in fast, and their very existence is at stake.

Once again, Timber leads the Grindlewood Army as they try to save the Wandeleis from destruction. In their scariest quest so far, the children and their pets have their courage and loyalty tested to the limit. They must do everything they can to protect Grindlewood and guard the Wandeleis' precious secrets from Zora, but they no longer know who they can trust.